Christopher Toppan Thayer

An Address Delivered in the First Parish, Beverly

Christopher Toppan Thayer

An Address Delivered in the First Parish, Beverly

ISBN/EAN: 9783337429485

Printed in Europe, USA, Canada, Australia, Japan

Cover: Foto ©Andreas Hilbeck / pixelio.de

More available books at **www.hansebooks.com**

MR. THAYER'S

BI-CENTENNIAL ADDRESS.

AN ADDRESS

DELIVERED IN THE

FIRST PARISH, BEVERLY,

OCTOBER 2, 1867,

ON THE TWO-HUNDREDTH ANNIVERSARY OF ITS FORMATION.

BY

CHRISTOPHER T. THAYER.

Published by Request of the Parish.

BOSTON:

NICHOLS AND NOYES,

117, WASHINGTON STREET.

1868.

ADDRESS.

My respected Friends and Auditors of this numerous Assembly, — As I saw this bright and genial October sun rise from its ocean bed yonder, my thoughts being occupied with preparation for these anniversary services, I was ready to recognize it as imaging Heaven's smile upon them. I could easily fancy it, in relation to them and their objects, illuming and bearing a benediction from the past, shedding a brilliant radiance on the present, and casting cheering beams into the future. And though here and there, even in the effulgence of this morning's rays, as in all human experiences and anticipations, —

> " A cloud I might behold,
> Hope played on its edges and tinged them with gold."

On this beautiful and chosen day we have met, to exchange mutual congratulations, and to indulge meditations on the past, the present, and the future, which may befit the introduction of a new century, — the advent of the third century in the life of this parish. That the occasion is one of no common interest, is attested by the large audience before me, composed not only of the parishioners and those more immediately concerned, but of others far and near who have afforded their countenance and sympathy. The mother church, the first in Salem, has here her representation, headed by one of her most able ministers, who at the same time is to be regarded as among her chief lay supporters and pillars, and whom I am most happy to regard as the friend of my youth, my life-long friend. The eldest daughter of this church, now more than a century and a half in age, the second in Beverly, is represented by various members, and especially by one with whom, as its pastor, I was for many years in public and private very cordially and agreeably associated. Representatives from all the other churches of the town the loving, and we trust beloved, mother hails at this time, and would gather them under her wings. One sadly I miss, — the lately deceased pastor of the Dane-street Church, the theologian, the scholar, the Christian gentleman, bearing a name and title familiar and dear in this parish, and in a much wider circle, — Dr. Abbot, with whom for more than twenty years I was intimately and happily connected in social intercourse, and in educational, reformatory, and other public concerns; and whose heart, however he might differ from us in faith or mode, I am sure would have been, rather I would say may be, with you and me to-day.

I could have wished that it might have been committed to some one abler and worthier to meet the demands of this occasion. The invitation to do so came to me when not quite in my usual health and strength, and when other engagements left me but brief space for complying with it. But coming as it did, with the unanimous vote of the parish to which I had so long, and so pleasantly to myself at least, sustained the pastoral relation, and accompanied with the expressed wish of the present pastor, it had to me the force of a mandate which I could not hesitate to obey. I confess also the desire to lay one more offering, humble though it be, on this altar, at which my early freshness and vigor were consecrated to the service of this ancient and honorable religious society.

I call it ancient, though we well know that is a comparative term. When we look at the peoples, nations, institutions, structures of the old, and even of the new world; when we see the splendid cathedrals in which our ancestors worshipped before they left their dear native land, and in which their forefathers for centuries had worshipped; when, as I have seen, plants and flowers are gathered from walls, such as those of the cathedral at Cologne, that for hundreds of years have been in building and not yet completed, — plants nourished and caused to flourish and bud and bloom by literally the dust of ages; when at St. Peter's in Rome we go down to the base, and explore the foundations on which a former temple had long rested, before the present, the most magnificent of modern times, was erected upon them; and when, further on, we gaze at the wonderful ruins of Pæstum, standing in solitary grandeur and massive proportions, yet steadily crumbling under the inevitable touch of decay, — we are reminded at once of the period when time had a beginning, and of that when it shall be no more: from such instances alone, we feel how comparatively brief are two centuries, even though they do cover the lives of six generations of men. But when we consider what is included in these last two, — those who have lived and acted therein, their institutions, revolutions, works, whether for good or evil; and how in this region the small seed here sown has grown and fructified, and that the little one has become thousands and millions, and before this century closes may be an hundred millions, — we realize, it may be imperfectly, that as —

> " One glorious hour of crowded life
> Is worth an age without a name," —

so it is grand and glorious to live within a space, longer or shorter be it rated, in which so much has been dared, experienced, and accomplished. And as wisdom consisteth not in length of days or years, so it is not the dim, hoar-frosted, irrevocable past, but the ages in which the greatest advances have been made in physical, social, intellectual, moral, and religious culture, by which true and real antiquity is to be measured.

I have termed our society honorable, as well as ancient. Such indeed I regard it. When I think of the noble character of the men and women by whom it was formed and has been sustained, my heart swells with veneration and gratitude toward them; and I could hardly say which of the emotions predominates. Its founders, so far as I can learn from its records and from contemporaneous history, were all honorable men. The two who took the lead in its formation were cast in no common mould, were

of nature's nobility. These were Roger Conant and Thomas
Lothrop, — the former styled, in the language of their day, "a
prudent, pious, and worthy gentleman;" and the latter, "a godly
and courageous commander." Conant may in truth be considered the patriarch, not only of this parish, but of this region
and the whole Massachusetts colony. Born in England, he
came over, in the prime of his manhood, to the then infant
settlement at Plymouth, entirely willing to carry on the "wilderness work" which had there been commenced, — fully prepared
to share the privations, trials, and struggles that attended its
beginning. Soon finding, however, that he differed in important
respects, or at least those so deemed, from the Plymouth colonists, he resolved on a change of residence. The main point
of difference was, that, while they were Separatists, — deter-
mined to wholly separate from the English Church, even to
abolishing the celebration of Christmas, — he was bent on free-
ing it of existing errors and corruptions, and adhering to its support. The element of his character thus revealed, — that of
mingled conservatism and liberality, — let me say by the way,
runs as a golden thread, and vibrates like a delicate, melodious
string, through the entire history of this parish. That such
should have been the case, it is not unreasonable to ascribe in
no small measure to the spirit by which its chief founder was
distinguished and actuated, and which would seem to have left its
impress on his own and many succeeding generations. From
Plymouth he went to Nantasket, now Hull, in Boston Bay; but,
after a brief stay there, he was appointed to act as governor of a
station established by an English company at Gloucester harbor,
Cape Ann, for fishing and trade. While discharging faithfully
the duties of this office, he evinced singular wisdom and power of
conciliation in the adjustment of difficulties that had arisen between some of his own company and another party headed by the
celebrated warrior, Miles Standish, and which seriously threatened to terminate in bloodshed. Meanwhile he had coasted up
and down the beautiful south shore of the Cape; agreeing, no
doubt, with Captain John Smith of Virginia memory, that it was
the "paradise of all these parts." It has indeed been justly com-

pared to some of the fine points on the Mediterranean. The view from the height above Mingo's beach bears a striking resemblance to that from Cicero's villa on the sea at Mola di Gaeta. Smith's first impression certainly receives a full indorsement from the prevailing current of taste and fashion.

Having met with some disasters, and regarding his position as one of temporary and commercial expediency, Conant decided to locate farther up the bay. The location on which he fixed is the neck of land on the south-west point of Beverly Harbor. To this he was induced, perhaps, by the considerations which are said to have influenced the first settlers of Boston, — that being peninsular, and connected with the mainland by a narrow isthmus, they might be the better protected from bears, wolves, and mosquitoes. And yet even now bears of some sort invade State Street, and exult or moan, as their case may be; and wolves, though possibly in sheep's clothing, may be found in Beacon Street, — and fortunate are the inhabitants who are exempt from the buzz and sting of the insects last named. In the autumn of 1626, he, with his little band, numbering not more than thirty in all, came, landing (tradition has it) on the rock west of the southerly end of Essex Bridge. Geologists term the stone "metamorphic," and find on it the marks of no less than eleven volcanic eruptions. Well — and with no irreverence surely — might we wish that the almighty Being, who in his wonder-working caused them, had, as a twelfth signature of his divine power, affixed the very footprints of the worthy company that first stepped on that rock, to make here their permanent abode. The rock of Plymouth, on which the forefathers landed, must ever retain its prominence, be, — as it were, the corner-stone of New England. It has been facetiously called our Blarney-stone. But for ever holy and hallowed will be the spot where first the Pilgrim fathers trod. Do not both that I have named, the one on the south and the other on the north shore of Massachusetts Bay, alike typify the solid foundations of learning, religion, and character, on which our Commonwealth is built? Literally, as well as metaphorically, may it be said to have been founded on a rock. Conant's principal companions in thus establishing himself were John Woodberry, John Balch, and Peter Palfrey. I take great pleasure in recognizing in the last name that of an ancestor of John G. Palfrey, who, by his efforts in Congress and his writings, did so much to expose, cripple, and eventually destroy the "slave-power," and by his literary and professional career, and especially his History of New England, has so illustrated and adorned her historic annals. As the acknowledged leader in this new enterprise, Conant immediately and with characteristic energy set about organizing his little colony. Scarcely, however, was this arduous labor begun, when an unexpected and trying emergency arose. An Episcopalian clergyman, Lyford, who had ministered to the settlers at Cape Ann, and afterwards, on the breaking-up of that settlement, to those of them whom he accompanied hither, having received a pressing invitation to remove to Virginia, decided on himself accepting it, and also strongly urged all the other colonists at Naumkeag, as this region was then called, to join him in so doing, which would have involved the entire uprooting of the settlement here commenced. Some, a few only, influenced largely by severity of climate, by dread of Indian hostility, of famine, and many and great privations, yielded to his persuasions. But on Conant (says Phippen's interesting and able sketch of him and his associates, styled "Old Planters," in the publications of the Essex Institute) they fell powerless, like arrows on a rock. It was then, indeed, that he assumed the attitude and bearing of a Christian hero; saying in substance, if not in so many terms, "Go every one of you that will. Though all else forsake, I will not forsake. Here is my foot planted; and here, God willing, it shall remain. Pleasant are the places on which our lines have fallen. Desert though they now be, yet shall they rejoice and blossom as the rose. Here, on this spot, will I watch and wait; assured that if you, one and all, depart, a larger and goodlier company will be gathered on these shores. Equally sure am I, that here the true and everlasting gospel shall be preached and propagated, and a pure and living church established; that here shall be founded an asylum for the persecuted and oppressed everywhere ; here the seeds of civil and religious liberty be sown, to spring up and flourish in rich luxuriance ; and here a way be opened for the advent of a great, free, prosperous, and happy people."

Toward the end of the summer of 1628, John Endicott arrived with what, in that day of small things, seemed a numerous company, and which, together with the previous residents, swelled the whole population to upwards of a hundred persons. Timely and valuable as was this acquisition of numbers, character, and resources, Conant immediately found himself involved in further and serious difficulties. With the new-comers came the intelligence that he was required by the proprietors in England, who had shortly before been re-organized, to relinquish his office into other hands. On this being announced, a storm of indignation burst forth that shook to its base the colony, still unsettled and insecure, struggling for mere existence, in dubious infancy that might result in life or death. His old companions and followers were reluctant, nay totally unwilling, to have their tried, trusted, and beloved leader thus summarily superseded. For a long time the controversy between the respective parties was warm and violent, so that Endicott was not, till nine months after his arrival, inaugurated as governor. That it did not proceed further, and reach extremes, is to be ascribed to the intelligence and high worth of their heads. Especially was it owing to the practical good sense, the mild temper, and genuine magnanimity of Conant, that an amicable adjustment was effected, and graver consequences were averted. And, as a memorial of this happy and auspicious result, at the suggestion, it is supposed, of the revered and sainted Francis Higginson, the Hebrew name Salem, signifying " City of Peace," was given to the place, now become historical, being well known in this and other countries, and counting by scores its namesakes scattered over all parts of our land.

Active and efficient as he was in securing this desirable consummation, he was not less so in supporting the new government. The " frame-house " he had built at Gloucester was, we may presume with his consent and co-operation, taken down, and carried to Salem, for the gubernatorial residence, a portion of which is still standing on the north-east corner of Washington and Church Streets. Waiving his Episcopalian partialities, if such yet remained, he, with others who joined him in forming this parish, was prominent among the founders of the First in Salem, — the first Independent Congregational Church gathered in America; that of Plymouth having been organized on the other side of the ocean. He joined with Endicott in extending a cordial welcome to Governor John Winthrop, when, in the summer of 1630, he arrived with his numerous fleet, bringing a large accession to the population of the province, and having with him the London Company's charter, with full power to administer it; that being thus transferred to our own shores, planted on our soil, and destined to undergo various modifications, till it should grow into the magnificent tree of liberty, from which have been and are to be gathered so rich fruits, and whose leaves shall be for the healing, peace, joy of all nations. Under Winthrop's and succeeding administrations, Conant held several offices of trust and importance, — such as deputy to the first General Court in 1634, and long afterward a member of the Land Board and justice of the Quarter Court, — besides taking a deep and active interest, individually and officially, in town and ecclesiastical affairs.

It was in 1630 that he and a few others passed over to form a permanent settlement on this — then known as Bass River — side; which they did on a line extending from the inner harbor to the cove next below, and in the very year in which the metropolis of our Commonwealth and of New England was founded. Associated with him in this undertaking were John Balch, John and William Woodberry, by the last of whom he was joined, nearly forty years later, in rearing this Christian church. The two brothers of the name of Woodberry have ever since been numerously and honorably represented by their descendants here and elsewhere. Having, with four other original settlers, received from the town of Salem a grant of two hundred acres of land each at the head of Bass River, Conant soon removed thither, and there passed the remainder of his protracted life, being engaged in agricultural pursuits when not occupied with public duties. His last appearance in public was at the head of a petition for a change of the name of this town, when he was more than eighty years of age. It is given in full in Stone's valuable History of Beverly, and is, in view of his advanced age, and the scenes through which he had passed, peculiarly touching. Its date is May 28, 1671, less than three years after the town was incorporated and named. He addressed it " to the honored General Court, consisting of Magistrates and Deputies," commencing with an affecting allusion to his early experience as a colonist, thus : —

" The humble petition of Roger Conant, of Bass river alias Beverly, who hath bin a planter in New England fortie years and upwards, being one of the first, if not the very first, that resolved and made good my settlement under in matter of plantation with my family in this colony of the Massachusets Bay, and have bin instrumental both for the founding and carriing on of the same ; and when in the infancy thereof it was in great hazard of being deserted, I was a means, through grace assisting me, to stop the flight of those few that then were heere with me, and that by my utter deniall to goe away with them, who would have gone either for England, or mostly for Virginia, but thereupon stayed to the hazard of our lives."

His first reason for a change of name is " the great dislike and discontent of many of our people for this name of Beverly, because (we being but a small place) it hath caused on us a constant nickname of *Beggarly*; " which sounds singularly enough to such as, having had opportunity for judging, believe with me that no population of equal numbers and duration has enjoyed a larger share of substantial comfort and prosperity than has fallen to the lot of them who, from the millionnaire to those of humblest means, here were born or have lived. His second ground for the alteration he petitioned for was, that all of the first settlers then surviving having come " from the western part of England, desire this western name of Budleigh, a market town in Devonshire, and neere unto the sea as we are here in this place, and where myself was born."

I will not forbear quoting one further sentence from the petition, as true as it was creditable to him : —

" I never yet made sute or request unto the Generall Court for the least matter, tho' I think I might as well have done, as many others have, who have obtained much without hazard of life, or preferring the public good before their own interest, which, I praise God, I have done."

The Legislature wisely and well declined the petitioner's prayer, but instead of a name provided a much more real and valuable substitute ; granting him, in consideration of his long service and great worth, two hundred acres of land. Much as we may respect the so natural and deep feeling with which, in the evening of life, his thoughts recurred to fatherland and his native place, we should be excused from equally admiring the taste which would have had the name he desired in exchange for the good old euphonious one, under which this town was incorporated, which it has hitherto borne, and I trust will ever bear. The latter was derived from a town, once the residence of John de Beverly, so long ago as the beginning of the eighth century of our era. It is noted for its ancient and grand minster, has a population of several thousands, and is pleasantly situated, amid beautiful surrounding scenery, in the eastern part of England. In visiting it, I saw much to interest, all the more from the associations I carried with me from its namesake. Tourists from this quarter cannot but be struck, and have somewhat of a home-feeling awakened, as in travelling through that section of country they meet and are saluted with familiar names of places, and find themselves in quick succession, for instance, in Cambridge, Boston, Lynn, and Beverly. While we may congratulate ourselves that the aged and venerable Conant failed to deprive the town of this last good name, we may rejoice, that, after the attempt, he enjoyed for years a boon far better than any thing merely nominal ; not consisting only or chiefly of lands bestowed in acknowledgment of his long-tried fidelity in the great work he undertook, and to the important trusts committed to him, — but rather in his own

calm, even temper, and kindly, devout, Christian spirit; in a
consciousness of duty, public and private, bravely, diligently
performed, in the respect and love by which he was universally
attended and followed. And when his long and useful earthly
career, eked out to its eighty-ninth year, was brought to a close,
and he was summoned to go up higher, there was mourning
sincere and deep for him, in many a happy home, secure and
flourishing; where, previously to his coming, untamed and un-
tutored savages, alone of all human beings, had their abode,
and hunted and warred, roaming through a desert and dreary
wild, and where before him no civilized or Christian man had
dwelt. Well may we, in view of this imperfect sketch, borrow
an appellation from the language of apostolic time and a later day,
and denominate him the angel and patron-saint of this church
and parish. Of his leading associate in their establishment
(Lothrop), I could not, in view of his sincere, upright, and honorable character, and restrained no less than moved by that, speak
in terms of extravagant eulogy. Brave and gentle, generous and
just, confiding, yet cautious and wise, of large estate for the
time, bountifully as skilfully administered, never sparing of his
own exertions, but always ready for every good word or work,
he had a rare and remarkable hold on the confidence and affection of the community in which he lived. Not sustaining in
strictness the paternal relation, he bore the best attributes, sym-
pathies, and adornments of the parental heart, — thus resem-
bling him who, having discharged in private the duties of a
loving and faithful parent to children not his own, came at length
to be universally acknowledged the Father of his country. He
was a father of the fatherless, the widow's friend and support,
and the helper of any who had none else to abet or plead their
cause.

As a military man, he had what seems, amid the hardships,
perils, severities, and fierce conflicts of war, an unnatural combination of qualities, which, if seldom, are sometimes seen, — of
gentleness and bravery, of stern, inflexible purpose, with kind-
ness and generosity, of unwavering determination with ten-
derest sympathy, of mild forbearance with exalted courage, of

persevering, unfaltering energy, with true magnanimity. Says one who, from thorough investigation, could be relied on, "He was the friend of all. I know not where to find a more perfect union of the hero and the Christian; of all that is manly and chivalrous, with all that is tender, benevolent, and devout."

His house was not only the abode of a liberal hospitality, but an asylum for the orphan and the distressed. As objects of his bounty arose and multiplied, his dwelling as his heart seemed to expand; and he who otherwise had been solitary was, in the exercise of his kindly spirit, surrounded by a numerous family. Among them who shared his fostering care was a younger sister, Ellen, whom he brought with him on his return from a visit to England, who fulfilled his fondest wishes, and to whom he was ever afterward as both father and elder brother. She became the second wife of the veteran schoolmaster, Ezekiel Cheever, who taught for more than seventy years, — the first part being distributed in terms of twelve, eleven, and nine years, respectively, at New Haven, Ipswich, and Charlestown; and the last thirty-eight passed at the head of the Boston Latin School, in which capacity he served, with harness on, when he died, and his own long account was rendered in to the Master of all, from whom — if we may venture the surmise — was heard the plaudit, "Well done, good and faithful servant." His powers were wonderfully retained to the end. The celebrated Cotton Mather, celebrated for his learning and lack of wisdom, for virtues that he had and virtues that he had not, whose entire course was eccentric, partaking more of the centrifugal than the centripetal, says, in grateful admiration and deserved eulogy on the decease of Cheever, —

"Although he had usefully spent his life among children, yet he was not become twice a child. In the great work of bringing sons to be men, he was my master seven and thirty years ago; so long ago, that I must even mention my father's tutor for one of them. He was a Christian of the old fashion, — an old New-England Christian; and I may tell you, that was as venerable a sight as the world, since the days of primitive Christianity, has ever looked upon. He lived, as a master, the term which has been for above three thousand years assigned for the life of a man.

> "He lived, and to vast age no illness knew,
> Till Time's scythe, waiting for him, rusty grew.
> He lived and wrought; his labors were immense,
> But ne'er declined to preterperfect tense."

To him, and such as he was, is it greatly owing that the school-house was here, from the first, reared by the side of the house of worship; that the teacher's profession has come to be regarded no less honorable than useful; and that "good learning"—a phrase signifying the promotion of all that is true, great, and good—has been current with us from the beginning; been made, as it were, the motto, and its meaning and spirit infused into all of our civil and literary institutions.

Lothrop having, in early manhood, emigrated from England, settled first in what is now the city of Salem; but, a few years after, he received a grant of land on this shore, near the Cove, where is a continuation of the most populous part of the town, and there fixed his residence for the remainder of his life. There he lived for about forty years, a model of fidelity to all his public and private relations. Nothing of the kind can exceed the charming picture of his domestic life which has been handed down to us, and been of late most skilfully and appreciatively drawn. To his ever-ready sympathy as a man, a neighbor, counsellor, friend, there is abundant witness. Various, almost innumerable, were the calls made on him for advice, for consolation, for attesting, drafting, and executing wills, for appraisal of estates, as trustee and guardian. For several years, he was deputy to the General Court; first from Salem, then from this town, and a selectman of it all the time after its incorporation till his death. This last office was sometimes dignified with the title of "townsman;" and comprehending, as it then did, the powers and duties of overseer of the poor, assessor of taxes, surveyor of highways, and police judge, without specifying others, we may conclude that it was no sinecure, and that its incumbent might have been entitled also the "man-of-all-work."

His interest and activity in ecclesiastical, were no less than in secular affairs. Soon after his arrival, when quite a young man, he became a member of the Salem Church, with which he continued for a long time to worship and commune. When, in consequence of the increased population on this side, and the inconveniences of distance and crossing the intervening ferry, it was felt that new accommodations must be provided for the worshippers resident here, he took an active part in all the measures which resulted first in temporary arrangements for religious services, and ultimately — though not till about twenty years after their inception — in the complete organization of this society. Toward its establishment and primitive prosperity, his character, so high, pure, trusted, efficient, and altogether worthy, greatly contributed, especially connected as it was in the general esteem with that of Conant, his elder companion in the undertaking. The characters of the two, taken together, constituted a tower of strength, and an indubitable pledge for the success, the stability, and spiritual growth of the embryo parish. That when absent on distant expeditions, and even amid the din and stress of war, he was not unmindful of his parochial relations, and of the ties, religious as well as social, which bound him to his home, is evinced by the fact, that on his return from the attack of St. Johns and Port Royal, where he held an important command, and the capture of which he materially aided, he brought with him from the latter place, now Annapolis, and presented to the parish, a bell, which had been in use on a friary there; which was the first of five successive ones that here, by their vibrations, have summoned to united devotion, have tolled the knell of departed spirits vastly outnumbering you who survive, and, in tones scarcely less solemn, marked from day to day the departing hours; have sounded out triumphs of peace and war; have intoned, as it were, great events, joyful or sad, which have occurred within the last two centuries.

But the end of all this life of activity, energy, and usefulness was drawing on. A fearful tragedy was at hand, in which he was to act the most conspicuous part, to suffer, and fall a sacrifice. King Philip, foremost of Indian chiefs in this quarter, subtle as powerful, had roused his own and neighboring tribes to the determination of desperate warfare, — of nothing less than a life or death struggle between them and the colonists. Consternation, wide-spread and terrible, prevailed. No sense of security, but, rather, awful dread of overhanging peril, pervaded every dwelling and hamlet. Tomahawk and scalping-knife; fire-arms borrowed by savages from their civilized neighbors, and plied with a deadly precision ; hopeless captivity, or deliverance from it solely by a cruel death ; the torch of conflagration and the devouring flame ; tortures indescribable, and hardly to be conceived, worse than death, and making it welcome, — these all, and more than these, were elements of the cup of horrors, of which our ancestors of those trying times were called to drink. Of that cup, the people of my native place, then amounting to between two and three hundred, drank to the very dregs. " Within the borders of New England," says her historian, " there is no more attractive spot than the site of the town of Lancaster," Mass. It was a favorite resort and abode of the Indians of its vicinity. Their principal village, the centre around which their wigwams were gathered, was on a gentle, southerly, sunny slope, at the fork of the two branches of the Nashua River, most favorable for fishing and hunting, while the surrounding rich alluvions afforded ample fields for the cultivation of Indian corn. That village was within the bounds of my paternal estate ; and there, down to a recent period, have been discovered relics of the aboriginal inhabitants. So, near by, and now included in the acres standing under the same name, is the site of the garrison, whose inmates, on the tenth of February, 1676, were either ruthlessly killed, or borne away miserable captives. Among the latter was Mrs. Rowlandson, wife of the first minister of the town, who, wounded and bleeding, was carried off, with a sick and dying child, but, after three months of horrid experience, restored to her husband and friends. Her narrative of that experience — so graphic, so circumstantial, so descriptive of the modes of savage life — was among my earliest readings, and left an impression vivid and never to be effaced. I remember well how that, together with local traditions and associations, fired my youthful imagination, haunted my thoughts and fancies by day and my dreams by night. A village sacked, fired, destroyed, all but annihilated; men, women, and children murdered, captives, tormented, or dispersed to wander houseless and homeless, — such was the terrible result of savage hostilities in my birthplace, and such the image they had left behind.

When, the summer previous to the scenes I have thus faintly sketched, a cry came from the remoter settlements of Brookfield and on the Connecticut River, that similar perils and calamities were impending over them, there were not wanting, in these the more populated portions, the men to lend a helping hand, who, instead of shrinking from the emergency, were, and showed themselves to be, fully up to the crisis. There was Major Simon Willard, of highly honorable descent and family, most honored in his own deserts, the first of the name in our annals, — settler of Concord, and afterwards resident of Lancaster and Groton, — the legislator, magistrate, judge, referee, universally confided in; next to the commander-in-chief commanding the militia of the province; with a line of descendants that would do honor to any name, among whom were two presidents of Harvard College, one of whom was among the most worthy and honored ministers of your own parish. He at seventy years of age, and Lothrop a chief captain under him at sixty-five, — such was the stern stuff of which the fathers of that day were composed, and such their real calibre, — buckled on their armor, girded themselves for the fight, and went forth to the battle, in which the fates of not the frontier alone, but the entire New-England people, seemed involved. Willard, by a forced march, and by his bravery and military skill, raised the siege, and relieved the beleaguered garrison of Brookfield. Meantime, Lothrop — who had raised a company of a hundred men in his county, that, from their being of the young and most promising, might well be styled its "flower," and who, from his varied experience and tried courage and valor, was of course to take command — pressed on, and joined the forces under Willard at Hadley. Being charged by the latter with the transport of supplies of provisions from Deerfield, he with his company was on the route thence, and, feeling no apprehension of immediate danger, they had laid aside their arms, and paused to regale themselves from the clusters of grapes which hung by the wayside, when the coveted fruit turned to ashes in their grasp, and its sweetness was changed to the gall and bitterness of death. Volleys from hundreds of savages in ambush were poured upon them, like lightning from a clear sky; their gallant and beloved commander fell at the outset; they fought bravely, as best they could with that pall of death over them; but few survived to tell the tale, which, from that time, gave to the little stream they were crossing, which proved to so many "the narrow stream of death," the sad name of Bloody Brook.

This catastrophe sent a thrill of terror and dismay through all the New-England colonies. Especially did the news of it come with appalling force to this county, from which its choicest flowers, "all culled out of its towns," and blooming so lately in manly beauty and strength, had been thus suddenly cut down and withered, as by an untimely, killing frost. Throughout its length and breadth, scarcely was there a village or hamlet left unscathed by this great calamity, —

> " No flock, however watched and tended,
> But one dead lamb was there."

More particularly, and with stunning effect, did the blow fall here, where, beside several that were deeply lamented, the fallen chief was best known, and for that reason most respected, trusted, and loved. Writers at or near the time do but express the feeling generally prevalent, whether in wider or more restricted circles; while they accumulate, almost without limit, the phrases descriptive of sorrow, agony, and horror, such as " a sad and awful providence," " a dismal and fatal blow," " a sadder rebuke of Providence than any thing that hitherto had been," " a black and fatal day," " the saddest that ever befell New England."

We know full well, after the experience of the past few years of dread civil conflict, what it is to have the young, the brave, and excellent, the highly educated and refined, the flower of our chivalry, — and no more real chivalry has the world witnessed, — go forth with the holiest inspirations of freedom, of love of

country, of allegiance to duty and to God, leaving to the loving
heart behind a heavy burden of anxieties and harrowing apprehensions, — many of them, alas! falling like the beauty of Israel
on her high places, many of them numbered among the "unre-
turning brave," buried where they fell, or returning, if at all,
only on their shields. More than thirty of your number, including your minister, in that crisis thus went forth on land or sea:
and, blessed be God! the most of them returned in safety; but
some there are who are mourned, and will continue long to be
deeply lamented, yet bequeathing the rich solace of their having beautifully and gloriously died for their country. Well,
therefore, may we somewhat comprehend the sacrifices made by
the early fathers, when, out of all proportion to any other drafts
made on our population for service in war, they met the awful
demands made upon them, and appreciate both the pain and the
magnanimity with which they gave up their dearest and best to
what they regarded their country's cause. Edward Everett, the
Cicero of our country and age, whom the Head of the nation
(our proto-martyr President, and Heaven grant he may be the
last!) announced at his decease as our "first citizen," said, in
conclusion of his eloquent address at the laying of the corner-
stone of the Bloody-Brook monument, with his own peculiar
felicity, "The 'Flower of Essex' shall bloom in undying remembrance, as the lapse of time shall continually develop, in
richer abundance, the fruits of what was done and suffered by
our fathers."

I have dwelt thus long — longer perhaps than my space of
time and your patience might properly allow — on the lives
of the two men most prominent in the formation of this parish.
Others there were well worthy of mention, and on whose qualities and worth I would gladly enlarge, that were instrumental
in establishing it on a firm and durable basis. But, while
omitting particular notice of them, let me for a few moments
call your attention to the larger view, in which they also will
be included, of the high privileges we enjoy, and the great
obligations we owe, through the ancestors from whom we are
descended, and the excellent of the earth by whom the founda-

tions of Church and State among us were securely laid. Not to name or enumerate the Plymouth worthies, but to limit our view to those who arrived within these waters, what a gathering of the true and faithful do we behold ! First came Conant and his company, of whom I need not further speak. Then followed the company of Endicott, the wise, upright, magnanimous, yet not devoid of human passions, as was shown when, fined forty shillings for a personal assault, he said, that, if the subject of it had been a better foe, he would have preferred to settle the difficulty on the spot by bodily conflict. Soon afterward came John Winthrop, the great and good, a master-builder in our edifice of state. Accompanying him were choice spirits, actuated by the highest motives, inspired by a sublime enthusiasm, not counting their lives dear, but encountering all perils, and ready to endure all sufferings, for conscience' sake. Among them was Lady Arabella Johnson, whose coming and fate furnish one of the most pathetic stories in all history or romance. High-born, accomplished, leaving a home of refinement and luxury, of high and wide privilege, " a paradise of plenty for a wilderness of wants," pining in health on the dreary and trying voyage, but never faltering in self-devotion and holy purpose, revived by the sweet-scented gales from these shores, but only stepping on them to find a grave, which, though marked by neither brass nor marble, is known to be almost within sight of the spot where we are assembled, and which, within a few weeks after her mortal part was consigned to it, was shared by her noble, devoted, and grief-stricken husband They, and those that were with them, afford some of the grandest examples of Christian heroism, self-devotion, and pious trust. Baptized they were as by fire ; yet they were baptized, I fully believe, into a purer faith and a higher life than the world had before known. Their very names are redolent with the odor of sanctity ; though dead, they speak ; and, ever since they lived, an elevating and hallowing influence has, in this community at least, been exerted by their lives and characters.

Much has been said and thought of the errors and defects of our forefathers. Doubtless they are chargeable with such, both light and grave. Among the lighter we may reckon the controversy, conducted at the time with great and serious earnestness, concerning the wearing of veils by women at public worship. Roger Williams had taken the ground that they should always in divine service be worn. But John Cotton, one Sunday morning, when this theory was apparently in the full tide of success, and practically adopted by the good women of Salem, preached against it with such cogency of argument and convincing power, that they all, with one accord, came out in the afternoon with unveiled faces and charms. It must be remembered, however, that every age has its peculiarities and trivialities, when viewed by succeeding ages; and that our wisest and most charitable course is to judge the past as we would be judged by the future. Illiberality and exclusiveness have also been charged on our ancestors, and surely not without reason. They banished heretics, hung Quakers, and permitted none but those of their own religious faith and fellowship to enjoy the right of suffrage, or be called freemen. As appears by the records of Essex County, Henry Herrick and his wife Edith were fined ten and eleven shillings, respectively (why the difference does not appear, unless on the presumption that the man, as of old, was tempted by the woman), "for aiding and comforting," in this very town, "an excommunicated person, contrary to order." Yet it is to be considered, that the fathers regarded the society they founded here as a separate one, entitled to its own peculiar rights and privileges, and planted themselves especially on their favorite idea of a Christian Commonwealth.

Great misapprehension, too, prevails regarding the laws they enacted. Some of them, clearly, were barbarous in their spirit and execution. Thus Phillip Ratcliffe was sentenced to be whipped, have his ears cut off, fined forty shillings, and be banished from the colony, for uttering malignant and scandalous speeches against the government and church of Salem. Sentence passed on one William Andrews, a mere youth, was, that for conspiracy against his master's life he be whipped, — probably in no slight degree, — and then committed to the not usually tender mercies of slavery. Nevertheless, the " Body of Libertics," the first code of laws adopted in New England, whose enactment dates back to the year 1641, was in some respects far in advance of its time. It was drafted by Nathaniel Ward, of Ipswich, author of "The Simple Cobbler of Agawam," who, before entering the ministry, had studied and practised law in England; and a most honorable monument it is of his ability, learning, humaneness, and far-sighted sagacity. To man-stealing it affixed the foulest stigma, by subjecting it to the penalty of death. Whipping of wives by their husbands — which the English common law has allowed and justified almost, if not quite, to this day, the only trial under it being that of the occasion and degree of infliction — Ward's code absolutely forbade, with the single exception, that such correction should be resorted to only in self-defence; and it made a near approach to the separation of Church and State, as now existing among us, by ordaining that no church censure should degrade or depose any man from civil dignity, office, or authority. Though bearing traces of the times in which it was framed, and marked by peculiarities of the people for whom it was intended and to whom it was adapted, " it shows " (says one who had mastered it thoroughly in all its provisions and bearings) " that our ancestors, instead of deducing all their laws from the books of Moses, established at the outset a code of fundamental principles, which, taken as a whole, for wisdom, equity, adaptation to the wants of their community, and a liberality of sentiment superior to the age in which it was written, may fearlessly challenge comparison with any similar production, from Magna Charta itself to the latest Bill of Rights that has been put forth in Europe or America."

Then, and above all, the fathers and founders of our churches and social state were inspired and actuated by a true, living, fervent, whole-souled devotion, — devotion to the heavenly Father's will, and the work given them to do. The very spirit of Christ, that consists in such devotion, and dwelt in him without measure, was with them, — shaded, it might be, by false theories and human imperfections, yet was with them and in them abundantly. Faith in God, in his felt presence, in his benignant and superintending providence, that he would guide them to higher light and broader and better ends than had previously been attained, — this was their continual strong fortress. As a wall of fire it was around them, amid the trials, hardships, and perils to which they were exposed. Sustained and animated by that, they built better than they knew, achieved more than they purposed, rose to heights of usefulness and influence exceeding their loftiest aspirations. Their works do indeed follow them, and shall follow them, attended by the benedictions of countless multitudes, in all coming ages.

But I must hasten to the mention of particulars more directly connected with our parish history. Owing to the inconvenience of crossing by boat or of travel by land, and the increase of population being felt to justify the movement, initiatory steps were taken in 1649 for establishing separate worship on this side the river, — the people here still retaining, as a branch of the same vine, their connection with the Salem parish, and those of them that were communicants joining in the communion service with their brethren across the water. A proposition to this effect was at first refused, for what reason it does not precisely appear. Evidently there was no desire of either party to be rid of the other, since the union implied in the proposal was kept up with mutual interest and harmony for near a score of years after it was renewed and granted. The arrangement proposed was entered into the next year after its inception. No house of worship was erected for the new congregation, till six years afterward when one was built on or near the site of your vestry. What its materials, dimensions, and style were, cannot now be ascertained. Probably it exhibited some improvement in material at least, if not in other respects, on the first Boston meeting-house, that stood on the east corner of State and Devonshire Streets; which was built a quarter century before, with mud walls and thatched roof, — though soon after, in consequence of a serious conflagration, it was ordered by the town that none should build there with thatched roofs or wooden chimneys. Modest, humble, and primitive in its construction and arrangements we may surely infer it was, when we read the records of

" liberty granted certain females wanting seats to build three at
their own charge;" of two male members having "leave to make
a seat at the north end of the pulpit;" and Mrs. Hale, the minister's wife, permitted "liberty to make a seat where she now
sitteth, it not being prejudicial to the rest;" that Mrs. Lothrop,
no doubt from the high esteem in which she, together with her
husband, was held, "had liberty to make a seat convenient by
the chief pillar;" that, it having been concluded to put up a gallery, the three parishioners contracting to do the work were to
"have each of them a seat in the foreseat." So late as 1672,
sixteen years after its erection, "it was agreed that the meeting-
house be ceiled up to the wall-plates, rabitted, and the windows
glazed." Yet this structure, humble as it was, less interesting
far than the hillsides of Scotland, where the Covenanters assembled and worshipped, repulsive even to our modern notions of
convenience and taste, was, notwithstanding, the cherished religious home of many a chosen and pious soul, — a temple consecrated in the hearts of simple-minded, true-hearted, devout men,
women, and children, to the worship of the Father in spirit and
truth. Beside this chief and highest purpose to which it was
devoted, in accord with their estimation of the school as an institution second only to the church, our ancestors gathered there
their youth, to be instructed in common, next to sacred, knowledge. There, also, they met from time to time, for the discreet,
patriotic, and faithful ordering of their civil affairs; not doubting,
but profoundly believing, that civil government was to be intelli-
gently, diligently, reverentially sustained, as being nothing less
than the ordinance of God. It had, moreover, the affecting
association, which belongs to so many of the churches of Old
and New England, of bordering on the place of graves, where
the mortal remains of near kindred and friends of the first worshippers reposed, where "the forefathers of the hamlet sleep,"
— your forefathers and mine. I say mine; for I trust you will
not think it amiss for me to recur with satisfaction to my descent
from Andrew Elliot, an emigrant from the west of England,
early a member of this parish and church, the first town-clerk
of Beverly; who discharged many offices of distinction and

trust faithfully and through a long period, sharing extensively the approbation and confidence of his townsmen and the community, and, besides his fair written records, leaving behind him the fairer record of his life.

Before and after the erection of the first meeting-house, temporary ministerial supplies were obtained, among them two of the name of Hubbard as recorded, more correctly Hobart; from one of whom the celebrated missionary, David Brainard, descended. Next came John Hale, who served here for three years previous to his being the regularly established pastor. He was a native of Charlestown, and graduated at Harvard College, when what is now called the venerable alma mater, the beloved mother of American colleges, and of so numerous and worthy — not to speak of the unworthy — sons, was comparatively in her infancy. He was the first of the eight who have here, on an average of more than a quarter century each, ministered in sacred things; first of the six of them that enjoyed her fostering care; while of the other two, not being myself one of them, I may be permitted to say that they have done no discredit, but greatly the reverse, to the highly flourishing and valuable institutions of Dartmouth and Amherst, at which, respectively, they had their early training. That all were what the fact of a collegiate education implies, — without assuming any thing more, — liberally educated, shows conclusively that here, from first to last, there has been no desire, design, or countenance of the divorce of learning from religion.

At length, the time seemed fully to have arrived for the ripened fruit to drop off, for the branch to be lopped from the parent tree and grafted on an independent stock. A score of years had passed since the separation had been agitated and been in progress, which, to us of this fast age, seems exceeding moderation. Moreover, it was felt by the residents on this side, not only that their convenience would be consulted, their attendance on the ordinances rendered more sure and uniform, and the edification therefrom better promoted, by a distinct parochial organization, but that in John Hale they had found "the able and approved teacher" whom the permission allowing them to set up separate worship authorized and required them to obtain, whose services as their pastor they desired to secure. Accordingly, this petition, headed by Roger Conant, was presented, signed by seventy-three persons, of whom two-thirds were church members: " We, whose names are underwritten, the brethren and sisters on Bass-River side, do present our desires to the rest of the church in Salem, that, with their consent, we and our children may be a church of ourselves; which we also present unto Mr. Hale, desiring him to join with us and to be our pastor, with the approbation of the rest of the church." On receipt of this petition, an appointed day, " by the consent of the brethren both on that side of the river and here at the town, was publicly observed as a day of solemn fasting and prayer, to seek unto God for his direction and presence in such a weighty matter." After mature deliberation on the subject so seriously viewed and acted upon, at a meeting held in 1667, July 4th (a day, when regarded from our stand-point, not inauspicious, though not then, as now, associated with ideas of either ecclesiastical or civil independence), " there was a unanimous consent of the brethren present unto their desire, only it was left to the sacrament day after, when in the fullest church assembly the consent of the rest of the church was signified by their vote, lifting up their hands; and so they have their liberty to be a church of themselves, only they continue members until their being a church :" with the added benediction, which doubtless was concurred in by all concerned, — " The Lord grant his gracious presence with them ! "

They were not slow to adopt measures for fulfilling the only remaining condition on which the liberty of separation was made to rest, — which was the thing itself they desired and had sought, — namely, a separate church organization. Yet they did so in no spirit of alienation or opposition ; rather that of those who, having passed the period of guardianship and pupilage, go forth from the shelter of the parental roof with alacrity and redoubled energies to the new spheres of duty and responsibility Providence has assigned them, yet without any diminution of filial and fraternal feeling, of tender, generous, and sacred sympathy, toward the loving and beloved circle left behind; those sentiments and emotions, on the contrary, being quickened, heightened, intensified, when the time arrives for relinquishing the constant and endeared intercourse of the native home.

An invitation in due form was now extended to Mr. Hale to be the pastor of the parish and church then to be organized· Considering it was virtually a triennial candidateship and experience of each other that had been gone through, — surpassing in duration a large proportion of the ministries of these degenerate days, — the invitation cannot but be regarded as highly honorable to both parties. His answer breathes a spirit of so calm and devout deliberation, such self-distrust, yet moral courage and trust in God, such self-devotion to the gospel and to the people whose religious teacher, guide, and friend he had so long been, under circumstances, some of which were singular and trying, that I am induced to recite it as it stands, — a relic no way discreditable to his memory, and curious as indicative of the modes of thought and expression peculiar to his time. It was as follows : —

"When I look at the weight of the work you call me unto, of which Paul cried out, 'Who is sufficient unto these things?' I then looking upon my manifold infirmities and indisposition of spirit, then unto so many discouragements; but, when I duly consider the Lord's sovereignty over me and all-sufficiency for my support, I desire, when I see his work and call, to say with Isaiah, 'Here I am: send me.' And in particular when I observe the remarkable providences of God in bringing me hither and paving out our way hitherto, and the room the Lord hath made for me in your hearts (which I acknowledge with thankfulness to God and yourselves), I also look at the call of God in the present call, as a call to me; being the more confirmed herein by the concurrence of our apprehensions, which hath appeared in those things we had occasion to confer about, concerning our entering into and proceeding with church affairs, which I hope the Lord will enable me to practise accordingly. Wherefore, while you walk according to God's order of the gospel and in the steadfastness of the faith of Christ, and I see that with a good conscience and freedom of spirit I can carry on my work, and discharge my duty to God and man and these that are under my care, according to the respective relation I may bear unto them, so long as the Lord is calling me to labor in this part of his vineyard, I desire to give up myself to the Lord and his service in the work of the ministry in this place; requesting you to strive together with me in your prayers for me, that it may redound to his glory, the edifying of every soul that shall dwell amongst us, and for our joyful account in the day of Christ's appearance. By me, JOHN HALE."

A pastor having thus been procured, the next object in view was to organize a church. For it should be understood, that the church strictly speaking, — that is, as composed of church-members, — had then a potential voice and a predominance of numbers and influence rarely if ever to be met with in our congregational churches at the present day. All along, as we trace the negotiations preceding the separation of ours from the parent society, we perceive it to be implied that the church was every thing, the parish little or nothing. This is shown by the mere name agreed on for the new body to be formed, — which was "the Church of Christ at Bass River in Salem," — no mention being made of the parish; though that may have been included in the designation, and may have been understood as resulting from the previous maintenance of separate worship. Fourteen months after their formation, the town was incorporated, and thenceforth they were called and known as the First Parish and Church in Beverly; the records and doings of the town and parish, as was generally the case where only one parish existed in a municipality, being extensively intermingled. Of late — indeed for a long time — the original order has been reversed, and the parish has been spoken of as including of course a church; and under its corporate title all parochial business of the society, consisting of persons within and without the church in its stricter acceptation, has been transacted. These two bodies, however, have here from the first been in great harmony. In one respect it may be confidently affirmed, that they have ever been in perfect agreement; which is this: Planting themselves, as both at the outset did, on the grand principle of their absolute independence of all foreign ecclesiastical control, they have been united by one spirit and the bond of peace in adhering to it without hesitation, wavering, or reservation; in carrying it in practice fully out to its legitimate conclusions; and, while loyally submitting to the civil law, acknowledging subjection to no other laws than those of conscience and of God. There is, too, a simplicity which to my apprehension is truly admirable, in the means employed by the founders of each, who were in fact mostly the same persons, to compass their chief aim, — the moral and religious improvement of their people. Uniting the offices common to both of pastor and teacher, which had elsewhere been kept distinct, they joined in the election of a single pastor or minister. Discarding the distinction that prevailed in other churches, between ruling elders and deacons, this church at the beginning elected simply the latter officers, from which course it has never since departed; having been served by upwards of twenty in that capacity. Dispensing with all offices, lay or clerical, that were merely honorary or titular, both parish and church have hitherto created and sustained, whether for regular or special purposes, such only as had a practical and intimate relation to the furthering of its appropriate objects, — as were deemed essential to the management of their prudential affairs, the raising, keeping, and expenditure of requisite pecuniary means, the distribution of charities, the support and right administering of religious ordinances and institutions, the maintenance besides of friendly and mutually edifying relations with other Christian associations. And these offices have been filled from the first by persons (I speak as becomes me of the departed only) on whose characters no recorded stigma rests, and on whose reputation for high respectability, intelligence, and worth, any religious community might justly be congratulated.

An important part in the preparation for establishing the church, and regarded indispensable by its founders, was the framing and adoption of a covenant. That which they agreed upon was simple, comprehensive, liberal, — from little of which we of our denomination should dissent. Coupled with it was a confession of faith, more stringent, Calvinistic, to a great deal of which Unitarians of all shades of belief could not subscribe. It is noticeable, that the earliest New-England church covenants were less restricted in doctrine and more liberal in spirit than many subsequently adopted, — some of them on the very spots where the former originally existed. Thus at Salem the first is ascertained to have been in these few expressive and pregnant words : " We covenant with our Lord and one with another, and we do bind ourselves in the presence of God, to walk together in all his ways, according as he is pleased to reveal himself unto us in his blessed word of truth." It is pleasant to know and realize, that some of the fathers here were foremost among the signers of this covenant, — so charmingly simple and concise, compressing so much of meaning within so little space, breathing so large a spirit of charity toward man and love to God ; harmonizing, too, so admirably with the saying of John Robinson, that God has much light yet to break forth from his holy word. Additions, nevertheless, were in no long time made to it, which, while multiplying articles of faith, abridged its breadth and freedom, and tended to narrow essentially the range of spiritual vision and feeling with any who might come under its binding power. So it was in the Pilgrim Church of Plymouth. When the late venerable James Kendall was about being settled there, he found a covenant in use and operation, to parts of which he could not conscientiously assent. He therefore prevailed on the members to restore the old first covenant on which that church was originally based, on which he had no difficulty in standing himself, or in admitting suitable candidates to membership. Various reasons may be assigned for this apparent declension in enlightened, liberal views and action. Among them, unquestionably, one not to be lightly considered or passed over is this, — the annoyance, dread, and hinderance occasioned in the ordering and carrying out of our ancestors' chosen mission, by the invading host of them whom they judged to be heretical and schismatic : such as the Brownes endeavoring to gain a foothold for Episcopacy, from which they had seceded and to which they were uncompromisingly opposed ; Roger Williams impugning not only their

5

doctrine of pedobaptism, but other deeply-rooted ideas of theirs on civil no less than on purely ecclesiastical matters; Ann Hutchinson, amid her divers eccentricities and assumptions, committing the unpardonable offence of declaring openly that the ministers in these parts preached " a covenant of works, and not of grace; " the Quakers also — hardly, cruelly as they were treated, persecuted and hanged, peace-loving, and not peace-disturbing, as their career on the whole has been — being then and here not literally Quietists, any more than they were of the sect of that name, that arose a thousand years before theirs, and was so called from esteeming quiet and inaction the acme of spiritual elevation and bliss. Neither should we leave out of the account the lust of domination, prevalent in all ages, over minds and consciences, which delights in lording it over God's heritage, which believes and suits its action to the belief that its own way is in that which all men should walk.

We come now to the consummation toward which the ardent wishes of the fathers of this church and society had long tended. The 20th of September, 1667, — corresponding, when allowance is made for the difference between the old and new styles of reckoning, almost precisely to the date, two centuries later, of our present assembling, — was fixed upon as the day for organizing the church, and for the ordination of its pastor elect. On that occasion, ministers and delegates were present, by invitation, from the neighboring churches of Ipswich, Wenham, and Salem. Of the attendance from the latter, say its records, " In regard to our nearness, and that they are a church issuing out of ourselves, it was thought meet for as many to be present as could; so, when the day came, divers of the brethren were present." First in order was the formation of the church, which is thus briefly described : " Mr. Hale propounded and read a confession of faith and covenant, which they had often considered amongst themselves, and did then (all that had been in full communion in the church of Salem) express their consent unto that confession and covenant, and so were owned as a particular and distinct church of themselves, by the messengers of the churches present." The service of ordination consisted in laying on of hands by John

Higginson, assisted by the two other ministers of churches then represented; and thus was fellowship given and received, and the newly-appointed pastor consecrated and publicly recognized. Going back in fancy, through the long line of two centuries, to that simple and touching scene, may we not, without undue stress of faith or imagination, trust that the benediction implored by him who led in the service — who, the worthy son of a sainted sire, not for his name alone, but for his pure, benevolent, devout spirit, was the St. John of his time in our churches — was the much-availing prayer of the righteous, drawing down blessings untold and immeasurable on the fathers and their descendants in the past and all coming ages ?

The ministry so auspiciously commenced lasted for the third of a century, with no interruption of the mutually happy relations of pastor and people. They were thoughtful and liberal, according to their means and the requirements of the times, in providing for the support and comfort of himself and family; and he was considerate, sympathizing, generous, faithful in public and private, toward them. Unbroken harmony of feeling and action appears to have prevailed between him and them; excepting in the single instance of his having been appointed chaplain in the military expedition against the French of Canada, in 1690, when, contrary to the expressed wishes of his parishioners, and their remonstrance before the General Court against the appointment, he decided on its acceptance. We cannot but admire, as they undoubtedly did, the courage and self-sacrifice which prompted him to confront and share the perils of that hazardous expedition through the wilderness, that he might guide and guard the citizen-soldiers composing it amid the scarcely less moral dangers to which they would be exposed, especially that he might comfort and strengthen the portion of it — forming a whole company, under command of Captain Rayment — which was enlisted from his own parish. After the lapse of nearly a century and three-quarters, his course and experience in that emergency come before us the more vividly, and sentiments of admiring and patriotic pride and gratitude are awakened anew, by the parallel furnished by your present pastor, in the recent struggle for national life, for civil liberty, for humanity's dearest rights and interests.

Notwithstanding the disturbing forces from without, particularly the wars with the French and Indians, in which a large proportion of the population was at different times engaged, and by which sad disaster and havoc were occasionally wrought, the parish steadily gained in numbers and strength, and so far grew and flourished, that it became necessary to erect the second meeting-house, which was completed in 1682, and stood on this spot. "This house, like the first, was used for the transaction of public business, and, beside the alterations and improvements made at various times, a powder-room was built in it for the safe-keeping of the ammunition belonging to the town. As fires at this time were never kindled in the meeting-house, it was considered the safest place to deposit powder. The sacredness of the place did not, however, allay the fears of the congregation, who left the house whenever a thunder-shower occurred." This structure, though in advance of the preceding and first one in form and convenience, was far from being what would now-a-days be regarded as very elegant or commodious. The exterior was in rude contrast with our modern notions of symmetry, adornment, and impressiveness. From the interior, all the beams and rafters, and the whole framework, were discernible. Tradition says there was whitewashing; but, from the sincere and earnest character of the builders, we may conclude that there was little of that, were it but materially. No paint or plastering, outside or within, relieved the plain, uniform wood-color. The belfry was on the middle of the roof, the bell-rope coming down into the centre aisle; on each side of which, and also in the gallery, were long benches for seating worshippers. What was the construction of the floor on which they rested, we do not precisely know, but may be sure it was not tessellated, or inlaid with precious stones or woods, — most probably was of ordinary planks, since, between forty and fifty years after the house was built, a floor was laid "upon the beams with boards and joist." As for the carpeting, warming, and appliances for decoration or comfort, to which we are accustomed, the mere suggestion of them would have been deemed by the builders a clear token of irreverence, levity, and coldness of heart.

"Seating the meeting" was with them a matter of special concern. As early as 1671, a committee of the parish was appointed, to be "joined with the selectmen, to seat all the married persons in the meeting-house;" from which it might be inferred, unjustly it is to be hoped, that there was indifference as to what seats the unmarried had, or whether they had any. Some systematic arrangement was obviously desirable and necessary, to avoid confusion, as well as to conform to the peculiar notions and customs of the time. The rules adopted for the distribution of seats underwent various modifications, till at length they were reduced to an exact and clearly-defined system. By this it was ordered, — and so curious a specimen is it of the aristocracy and gallantry, no less than the simplicity and quaintness, that reigned in the period of which I am speaking, that I am tempted to quote its provisions; which are —

"That every male be allowed one degree for every complete year of age he exceeds twenty-one; that he be allowed for a captain's commission twelve degrees, for a lieutenant's eight, and for an ensign's four degrees; that he be allowed three degrees for every shilling for real estate in the last parish tax, and one degree for every shilling for personal estate and faculty; every six degrees for estate and faculty of a parent alive, to make one degree among his sons, or, where there are none, among the daughters that are seated; every generation heretofore living in this town to make one degree for every male descendant that is seated; parentage to be regarded no farther otherwise than to turn the scale between competition for the same seat; that taxes for polls of sons and servants shall give no advancement for masters or fathers, because such sons or servants have seats; that no degree be allowed on account of any one's predecessors having paid towards building the meeting-house, because it had fallen down before now, but for repairs since made; that some suitable abatement in degrees be made, where it is well known the person is greatly in debt; that the tenant of a freehold for term of years shall be allowed as many degrees as half the real estate entitles him to, and the landlord the other half; that the proprietor of lands in any other parish shall be (if under his own improvement) allowed as much as

he would be if they lay in this parish, but, if rented out, only half
as much; married women to be seated agreeably to the rank of their
husbands, and widows in the same degree as though their husbands were
yet living; that the foremost magistrate seat (so called) shall be the
highest in rank, and the other three in successive order; that the next
in rank shall be in the foremost of the front seats below, then the fore-
seat in the front-gallery, then the fore-seat in the side-gallery; that
the side-seat below shall be for elderly men, the foremost first or highest, and the others in order; that the seats behind the fore-front seat
below shall be for middle-aged men, according to their degree; that
the second or third seats in the front and side galleries shall be for
younger men, to rank the second first, and the third next."

Males were separated from females in location, and seats were
assigned to the latter, corresponding to the rank fixed for them
by the rules just stated. A grave objection to this arrangement
was the separation of the children and youth from the parents,
their natural guardians and regulators. Here the boy-genus was
— what in all ages and states of society I suppose it has been
found to be — a serious element of disturbance. Children were
mostly disposed of on benches in the aisles, or on the stairs. A
portion of the boys, including, it may be presumed, the most
unruly, were placed on the pulpit staircase, where they were
under the eye of the minister and exposed to the gaze of
the whole congregation. But this did not suffice to prevent
or suppress insubordination in this least interesting part of the
human creation. Such was the alarming height to which juve-
nile misdemeanors in the midst of divine service had attained,
that the town authorities were led to deliberate and take sum-
mary measures respecting them. At one time it was "ordered
by the selectmen, that the hinder seats of the elders' gallery be
altered, and the boys are to sit there, and Robert Hubbard to
have an eye out for them; and for the first offence to acquaint
their parents or masters of it, and, if they do offend again, to
acquaint the selectmen with it, who shall deal with them according to law." Another time the town — being then, as to such
matters, in all but name the parish — voted, "That the selectmen make such orders as convenient for the prevention of boys

and idle persons from sitting in such places, in our meeting-house, wherein they are out of public view, and so, in time of public worship, spend much of their time in play and disorder." By no means let it be understood that the evil was confined to the limits of this parish. Our Salem mother, staid and venerable as she might have been expected throughout to be, endured the same affliction. There, in 1676, an order was passed, " that all the boys of the town are and shall be appointed to sit upon the three pairs of stairs in the meeting-house on the Lord's day ; " and two persons were appointed to the charge of them, — one " to look to the boys that sit upon the pulpit stairs," the second " for the other stairs, to look to and order so many of the boys as may be convenient, and, if any are unruly, to present their names, as the law directs." Very many, not to say all, other parishes, before and ever since, have in like manner been troubled and tried by their " coming men."

For various well-known purposes, especially for the right ordering of the sanctuary, the office of sexton has, from time immemorial, been considered essential. The dread presence of that official, in particular when acting as tithing-man, will be remembered by not a few, in looking back to their youthful days, and might now often be needed, and be of salutary effect. Whether the duty of watching the drowsy worshippers and keeping them awake, which in some places was required of some one, devolved on him, does not precisely appear. But the turning of the glass specially belonged to him. An hour-glass was placed in a position where it could be observed by all present. Just as the sermon commenced, the sexton turned the glass. " If the minister completed his discourse before the sands had all run out, he was admonished that he had not complied with the reasonable expectations of his hearers, whether sleeping or waking, — both classes having tacitly contracted for an hour's enjoyment in their own way. If his zeal inclined him to go beyond the standard measure, the turning of the glass by the faithful sexton reminded him that he was asking more of the patience of his hearers than they had tacitly agreed to give. But instances were not rare in those days, when long sermons were less alarming than in this age of dispatch, in which, as has been facetiously remarked, both preachers and hearers were well content to take a second, and even a third, glass together." By the substitution of clocks (to which, it is to be feared, eyes of weariness, more than of delight, now turn), if not before or otherwise, this custom has long since ceased; and so the sexton's office was shorn of one of its chief distinctions. That office in this parish, for more than two centuries, has been filled by only seven individuals; it might almost be said by six, one of them having, within less than two months after he was appointed to it, dropped dead while ringing the evening bell. Of the first, the high praise is recorded, that, after a twenty years' service, it was required of his successor "that he should do, in all respects, as Goodman Bailey had done;" and that he fulfilled the requirement we may infer from the fact, that he continued in office for over sixty years. The last sexton has served a quarter of a century, and is still active and useful in the performance of his duties. Many of us remember, with sincere regard and regrets, Thomas Barrett, his immediate predecessor, who officiated for about fifty years, — who was ever so orderly and punctual, so respectful and reverential, so thoughtful and kind toward the living, so tender of the dead. Few more than he could truly and from the heart say, " I love the habitation of thine house : how amiable are thy tabernacles unto me, O God!" Seldom have I been more touched than when I saw his funeral procession wind around the front of this temple, which he had loved and served so well, and, entering the ancient first burial-ground, pass to the only vacant space for a grave; which, long before, he had reserved for himself, that he might be buried by the side of the wife of his youth.

Music has from the first been here made an important part of public worship. Very different, indeed, have been the styles in which it has been performed. "Deaconing" the psalm was that which prevailed in the primitive and several succeeding ages. It was so termed because the " musical exercises of the sanctuary, according to the custom of the times, were conducted by one of the deacons, who officiated as chorister to the congregation. He read the hymn, line by line, and set the tune, in

which each member joined by rote, in key and measure not
always the most exact or harmonious." Various were the modifications this custom underwent. In 1764, it was voted, that
singers be selected, and seated together, " that the spirit of singing psalms might be revived, and that part of worship conducted
with more regularity." Ten years later, the parish voted to
locate the choir in the front gallery, opposite to the pulpit, and
constituting a sort of correlative department with that, and commissioned with full powers " to pitch the tune and take the lead
in singing." Such changes were not effected in this generally
esteemed important matter without serious discussions and conflicts of opinion, and even strenuous resistance. Similar difficulties
and controversy existed in regard to the collections used in the
singing. Thus when, a century ago, Watts's Psalms and Hymns
were introduced in place of the antiquated version previously in
use, one man at least was so strongly moved as to take his hat,
and walk hurriedly out of the assembly; not quite so formal
and dignified a protest as that which, on a like occasion, at a
later period, was entered against what by some (and not a few)
was considered an alarming and monstrous innovation, — an aged
member of the second parish in this town rising amid its worshipping congregation under high excitement, and asserting, with
utmost gravity and earnestness, that, if Solomon had beheld
what they had then seen and heard, far from him would it have
been to say, " There is nothing new under the sun." After an
experience of more than a half century here, during which it
was felt by many, that, admirable and excellent as is much of
the devotional poetry of Watts, there is also much that accorded
with neither their views nor taste, a change was imperatively
demanded. Still there was a respectable minority, unwilling to
have the book, with which were linked such hallowed associations, superseded and banished from the sanctuary. Therefore
a compromise was agreed on, by which the Watts' collection was
to be used alternately with another (the West Boston one),
which, while retaining some of the best in the former, omitted
the most objectionable. But this, like most compromises, resulted fatally to the yielding party; the giving up of a part

having been soon followed by a concession of the whole, and the old supplanted altogether by the new. Any changes since made in your psalmody or hymnology, being such as were required by progress in intellectual and literary culture and devotional sentiment, have been accomplished with little or no agitation or dissension. And as for your choir, from its first institution, charged with giving voice and expression to the words of poets, inspired and uninspired, it has had less of the discord, in feeling and action, naturally expected from the association of a delicate and sensitive organization with musical taste and skill; while, composed as it ever has been almost entirely of your own members, among them some of the most respectable and worthy, as well as gifted and proficient in the science of sweet sounds and grand harmonies, they have not failed of their high duty of ministering, for themselves and others, to the sacred melody of the fervent and devout heart.

Witchcraft, or rather notions and practices relating to it, constituted a chief disturbing element in this society's first age. While the tempest, which demonology had from all times and lands, and the four winds of heaven, been gathering, burst in the immediate vicinity, this place must of necessity share in the wreck and ruin wrought by one of the direst commotions that ever raged in a community with any pretensions to being termed civilized or Christian. As we review the authentic accounts of the great drama enacted in 1692, with its reign of terror and awful tragedies, a nightmare seems upon us; and we pass, as it were, through a horrid dream. Ishmaelitish, in fact, a large portion of the people of this region had become, — their hands against every man, and every man's hand against theirs. Some of the strongest bonds by which society is held in unity, peace, and order, appeared about to be dissolved, and its very existence to be in jeopardy, — threatened with fast-approaching dissolution. Panic, mutual accusations, arrests, imprisonments, prevailing distrust and jealousies, wide-spread and untold anguish in individuals and families, the whole vast mass of misery and evil resulting from what we feel justified in pronouncing the witchcraft delusion, were not confined to this particular neighborhood. Elsewhere, scarcely less than in this devoted locality, the social fabric reeled and rocked on its apparently insecure base. Andover caught the contagion, having been visited by some of the propagators of the delusion direct from the district peculiarly infected: and a visitation truly it proved, not of angel strangers, but their opposites in human shape; and their visit did indeed cost dear, being followed by some of the worst calamities growing out of the scourge they brought. Prisoners by the hundred were lodged in jails, not in Salem only, but in Ipswich, Boston, and Cambridge. There they were immured in damp and loathsome cells, enduring grievous privations, looking back with harrowing regrets to the homes from which they had been torn, the friends from whom they had been abruptly and cruelly sundered, and forward with dreadful anticipation of capital trials, in which just and established rules of evidence, with the principles on which they are founded, would be ignored or set at nought; in which the most trivial, irrelevant, and absurd testimony would be freely admitted, and, in short, conviction of guilt be a foregone conclusion. The first victim of such trials — and, with such, truth obliges us to class the Salem trials for witchcraft — was Mrs. Edward Bishop, a member in full communion with this church. She was a woman of marked peculiarities in manners, style of dress, and mode of living, and quite independent of the opinions and fashions of her time. One of the witnesses against her "mentions, as corroborative proof of Bridget Bishop's being a witch, that she used to bring to his dye-house ‘sundry pieces of lace,’ of shapes and dimensions entirely outside of his conceptions of what could be needed in the wardrobe, or for the toilet of a plain and honest woman. He evidently regarded fashionable and vain apparel as a snare and sign of the Devil." If such proofs were still held to be allowable and convincing, they would bear hardly on many fine ladies of our day, who would thus be shown to be in a league, of which they could not be supposed ambitious to form a component part. Eccentric, self-reliant, firm in asserting and maintaining her rights, and, if need were, — as sometimes happened, — courageous in resisting interference with them, Mrs. Bishop's character had those salient points on which a persecution, mainly composed of superstition, fanaticism, vanity, spiritual pride, personal hostility, and private vengeance, was exactly adapted to fasten. Accordingly, at different times in a series of years previously to her final accusation and arraignment, she had been charged with egregious offences, especially with that most heinous sin of having conspired with Satan against the peace and welfare of mankind in general, and of God's elect in particular. She had, however, continued in regular standing with this church; and had been sustained and exculpated, under the heavy charges brought against her, by the members, including the minister, up to the time of her arrest by civil process. Among the saddest of stories is that of the closing scenes of her life, which yet may be told in a single and not very lengthened sentence. Dragged from her domestic retreat, with its appliances and comforts; brought into the crowded assembly; confronted there on the one hand by the examining magistrates in solemn state, and on the other by her false and infatuated accusers; on the wretched pretences there made committed to a dungeon; borne thence, solitary and alone, through streets thronged with a promiscuous multitude of the horror-stricken, the sad (some wisely sad), and the jeering and scoffing, to the court, where on testimony mostly frivolous, none of it relevant or well-substantiated, she was condemned to an ignominious death on the scaffold; and which having suffered, she was buried at the foot as it were of her cross, — all this, passing and endured within a few swiftly-fleeting weeks, into which were crowded the excruciating agonies of months and years. Thus passed away and perished one, a sincere, high-spirited, and Christian woman, whose blood has since flowed, and continues to flow, in the veins of some of the oldest and most respectable families in this vicinity. Thus perished the first of the twenty who — in that day, darkened by delusion and superstition of deepest dye, who, protesting uniformly conscious innocence — laid down their lives, and left their bodies to be deposited amid the crevices of the rocks, and scantily covered by earth, in the place of execution. On the rocky height selected for the purpose, and known by the interchangeable names of

Witch and Gallows Hill, with a grand surrounding expanse of town and country, sea and land, it may have been intended to set up a beacon of warning against all demoniacal approaches, wiles, and machinations; but, if it were a light set on a hill, it was one that shone with an ominous, a lurid, dismal radiance, and was wholly destitute of a cheering beam or genuine spiritual illumination.

One of the aggravating circumstances in the bitter experience of the first sacrifice to that mockery of justice, the Salem trials for witchcraft, was, that her own minister, who on former like occasions had stood up for her defence and succeeded in her rescue, testified at the last against her, and thus effectively aided in sealing her deplorable fate. For his conduct in this case, and the general countenance he gave to the delusion when at its height, Hale has been the subject of strong animadversion, — been charged, indeed, with gross inconsistency. Judging, however, from the character accorded to him by his contemporaries, for integrity, for high and varied excellence, I incline to believe that the inconsistency, apparent or actual, involved only the effects of the overshadowing and controlling power of theoretical error and sympathetic excitement, not of intentional wrong. But if the discernment and wisdom, attributed to him by some of the leading minds of his time, for a while were overborne and deserted him, the scales were soon made to fall from his eyes, and many beside his, by the evil being brought home to his own door. Perhaps the extreme had been reached, from which a recoil was inevitable. However that may have been, the re-action, whether begun then or before, was greatly accelerated when accusations were pointed at Mrs. Hale, whose superior worth was acknowledged and highly appreciated, as it was widely known. The commotion subsided by an almost instant collapse. Accusers became the accused. Those lately leaders were in their turn cried out against, and reproached in no measured terms as deceivers, by the deluded. Judges were severely judged, — some of them, like Sewall, coming out and manfully confessing the egregious errors into which they had fallen. Others there were who — instead of being incensed, or prompted to attempts at self-justification, by the reproaches heaped upon them as the aiders and abettors of the delusion, and therefore authors of so much mischief and suffering — set calmly and humbly about a review of the whole subject, taking for the guidance of their search the combined lights of experience, philosophy, and religion. Prominent among such was John Hale. Several years after the convulsions and horrors of 1692 had passed, when the excitement attendant and consequent on them had been allowed sufficient opportunity to subside, he published the results of his investigation in a small volume, highly commended at the time, and bearing the stamp of an intelligent, candid, earnest spirit. In that he takes distinctly the ground, that the witchcraft prosecutions were pushed to unjustifiable extremes. His reasons in reply to the question, "How it doth appear that there was a going too far in this affair," certainly have point and force. Briefly they are these: The great number of the accused, the quality or character of several of them, the number (fifty at least) of the afflicted, unqualified denial of guilt by all who were executed, and finally that Satan had been chained, so that accusers and accused had been quiet, for the five years and more that had elapsed since the last of the trials.

That book was shortly followed by another, which had great influence in enlightening and settling the public mind, — prepared by a Boston merchant, Robert Calef, and entitled "The Wonders of the Invisible World." Its spirit, far from being calm, gentle, reserved like the former, was free, outspoken, with a strong admixture of the indignant. He speaks without hesitation or qualification of the chief actors in the tragic scenes, which were then fresh, and bitter as they were fresh, in the recollection of multitudes, as "these criminals and their bloody principles." His summing up I give in substance, and nearly in his own language: —

"As long as Christians, real or nominal, deem the law of the Lord imperfect, not describing in this matter the crime punishable with death; the Devil a power above and against nature; the witches to commission him; the Devil's testimony to be preferred, invariably

and whatever the trustworthiness of the arraigned, to their plea of
not guilty ; life and liberty depending on confession of guilt ; that
the accused should undergo hardships and torments ; teats for the Devil
to suck be searched on the body as tokens of guilt ; the Lord's prayer
to be adopted, in a manner by which it is profaned, for a test ; witchcraft, sorcery, familiar spirits, necromancy, with many other proofs
alike fanciful and frivolous, to be used in discovering witches, —
while such things, that had been lately witnessed, and the effects of
which were far from having died away, are believed, said, and
done, so long it may be expected the innocent will suffer, God be
dishonored, and his judgments contemned."

Cotton Mather, incensed at the rough handling this little book
gave him and his coadjutors in promoting the witchcraft delu-
sions and persecutions, was betrayed by his indignation into
exclaiming, with one letter dropped from the name of its author,
" that Calf." There is a copy of the volume in the Massachusetts Historical Society's library, which once belonged to Mather
himself, in which, on the inside of the cover, is quoted in his
own handwriting, from the Book of Job, the passage, " Would
that mine adversary had written a book ! surely I would take
it upon my shoulder, and bind it as a crown to me." An adversary of his Calef clearly was, — an opponent not wholly
free from acerbity, because, with enlightenment on the subject
he treated, superior to most of that of his age, he smarted under
a sense of the errors, misdeeds, and cruelties of any and all
engaged in bringing on, keeping up, and heightening the delusion. But the quotation just repeated, and under the circumstances made, would seem a *lucus a non lucendo*, — the accepted
phrase for denoting words used to signify the opposite of their
literal or derivative sense. At any rate, the wish so expressed
by Mather he might, were he among us and so far as his credit
for wisdom and right conduct is concerned, gladly reverse,
making it to run thus : " Would that my friend had not written a book ! " — in view of one recently issued, in which, with no
other than friendly feelings, but with the higher love of truth,
the shameful part borne by him in fostering the delusion and
pursuing its victims is faithfully depicted. I refer, it hardly

needs be said, to Upham's "History of Witchcraft," — a work truly admirable for the thorough research, and the varied and extensive learning it displays, for its elegant and captivating style, its vivid and fascinating descriptions, and above all the practical value of its teachings, — leaving little to be desired, and still less to be anticipated, from future gleanings in the field surveyed.

I have been led further into this subject than at first contemplated, by the important bearing it was found to have on the early history of this parish, — entering largely into the opinions and feelings, the customs, habits, and experiences, of its people, involving the sacrifice of the life of one at least, and disturbing the peace and jeopardizing the lives of many, of its members. Its first minister, we have seen, was extensively implicated in the responsibilities, and connected with the scenes of persecution and horror, which arose amid the distractions of the time; and creditable as in some respects was his course in that day of severe trial, in others it required, if not censure, to be explained, and, as far as might be, vindicated. The position of his wife throughout, and especially in the climax of the fanatical excitement, was most honorable to herself and her sex. May we not rejoice, with something of local and parochial pride, that one of the sorest plagues with which humanity was ever visited, should have been in no small degree stayed and turned back by the delicate hand, the gentle spirit, and recognized virtues of that noble, Christian woman? From examples like hers we may learn the great lesson, that there is no power on earth to be compared with rectitude and conscious virtue, either in resisting temptation, and, as the strong language of Scripture has it, "in quenching the fiery darts of the wicked;" or in standing calm and firm, undaunted and unharmed, amid the tumults and rage of the people. And there are other lessons, which we of this age and all ages may well draw and apply with close self-application. They spring up and present themselves at the most impartial review of the ground which we have just traversed. While we view with unqualified admiration the grand and lofty position taken and sustained by some, among them the leading and largest minds, in that war of spiritual elements; whilst we admire, if possible yet more, the moral courage of those who suffered death, facing a cruel, wretched, and ignominious fate without dismay, meekly submitting themselves to the wrath of man and trusting to the mercy of God, who, they felt, knew and would attest the sincerity of their protested innocence, — not doubting, it might be and we trust was, that their posterity would not withhold from them the meed of simple justice and tender compassion, — while we behold this bright side of the picture, — for, notwithstanding the thick and dark clouds around, it was gloriously bright, — we must not, cannot, shut our eyes to that black one, from which issue ever-sounding voices of solemn warning. They warn us against the sin, the dangers, and evils of deception. No inquirer, though but moderately enlightened and candid, it seems to me, can doubt that gross deceit was the chief, I had almost said the sole, of the witcheries practised in those times that tried souls and witches together. Collusion went hand in hand with delusion. Mr. Parris, the minister of Salem village, now known as Danvers, in which the proceedings against witches originated, unless awfully belied by contemporary and subsequent accounts, was no inapt pupil in the school of the arch-deceiver; following, if not with equal steps, at no commendable distance, —

> " 'The first
> That practised falsehood under saintly show,
> Deep malice to conceal."

Then there were young girls and women, who, beginning with the practice of magic arts that were regarded innocent, quickly degenerated into death-dealing ones. Whatever the palliating circumstances which may be arrayed in their favor, it is evident they were to no small extent possessed and actuated by the foul spirit of deception. Against that in its very beginnings, the evil, which, led on by it, they wrought, speaks trumpet-tongued to old and young, and to all of every age, saying, in the strong utterance of the poet, —

7

> " What a tangled web we weave,
> When first we practise to deceive !
> Sincerity, thou first of virtues. Let
> No mortal leave the onward path,
> Although the earth should gape,
> And from the gulf of hell destruction cry,
> To take dissimulation's winding way."

We are warned also, by the memorable and tragic events alluded to and thus faintly sketched, against the perils and bad consequences of superstition and fanaticism. A great mistake it would be to suppose that these disturbing and dangerous causes had died out, or had ceased to operate. Existing tendencies, even in these modern times, show but too plainly that they need to be assiduously watched and guarded against. In respect to them, no less than to freedom, eternal vigilance is the price of security. If the beginning of strife is as when one letteth out water, which from the small stream soon grows to the torrent mighty to deluge, lay waste, and destroy; so fanatical passion may in the outset be the little fire which shortly kindles into a great conflagration, and becomes a vast, devouring element. "Of all things," says Burke, "wisdom is the most terrified with epidemical fanaticism, because, of all enemies, it is that against which she is least able to furnish any kind of resource." And the *rationale* of the matter is plain. Reasoning with passion, as such and alone, what is it but undertaking to reason with one both deaf and blind, that will not see or hear to reason ? Nothing can be more unsatisfactory and utterly vain. Therefore, while we admit freely the sacred obligation to keep our minds and hearts open to all of light and holy influence that may come from this world or another, and from all worlds, it becomes us to watch, with vigils always awake and active, against the passionate fires lighted and fed by superstition, fanaticism, or error of any sort, and to let our zeal for the truth, and the right even, be tempered by moderation, at the same time that it is, as it should be, ever-living and fervent.

But the storms of fanatical excitement, and of war with savages and civilized men, had subsided, when, in May, 1700, the primeval epoch of this parish was closed, and Hale, its first minis-

ter, sank peacefully — honored, beloved, deeply lamented — to
his final earthly rest; yet not without leaving a posterity to bear
up his name and nobly transmit his worth, some of whom we
gladly welcome here to-day, to aid in this commemorative service. He was succeeded, the following year, by Thomas Blowers, who was highly esteemed for his learning and virtues, and
particularly for his devotedness to the duties of his profession.
When a plan was set on foot by some of the leading ministers
of the province to consociate the churches, and thus curtail
their individual freedom, Blowers stood up manfully among the
foremost to resist what he viewed, as we certainly do, an at-
tempted usurpation of ecclesiastical authority. That attempt,
which then was effectually foiled, was renewed early in the
present century in our State, only to be again and alike unsuc-
cessful. He also distinguished himself by sustaining the election of Leverett to the presidency of Harvard against strenuous
opposers, who planted themselves mainly on the ground, that
the incumbent of that office should be selected from the clergy,
and not from the laity. By so doing, he did good and effective
service, and likewise manifested a wise and true liberality. His
departure, in the midst of his usefulness and the twenty-eighth
year of his ministry, was felt and mourned as a heavy loss and
bitter personal bereavement in this and the neighboring parishes.
From the strong hold he had, on not only the respect but affectionate attachment of the generation with whom and for whom
he lived and labored, of which the tradition, after the lapse of a
century and a half, is still fresh among us, he appears to have
been regarded, in a wide circle here and elsewhere, as a model
minister of his time, loving and greatly loved. Chief-Justice
Blowers, of Nova Scotia, long the oldest surviving graduate of
Harvard, who died in 1842, at the age of a hundred years, was
his grandson. His memory is brought visibly, as it were, before
us by his legacy of one of the most ancient silver pieces of the
communion service, which, including precious memorials of other
worthy donors, you have done well to spread at this time on the
Lord's table, guarded on either side by those whose office it is

to keep them and distribute their consecrated contents; thus recognizing simple truth, not mere fancy, in the words, —

> "The saints below and saints above
> But one communion make;"

and linking memories of departed benefactors and friends with the remembrance of him, whom, above all that have lived on earth, we are bound to remember with grateful reverence and love, — the Lord and Master who loved us with a love stronger than death.

The parish, too, has from time to time had its benefactions to recollect and acknowledge. Every one, however limited his means or small his contribution, who contributes of his substance toward upholding it and enlarging its usefulness, is to be accounted its benefactor. Still more is he such, and deserving to be mentioned as such, who, however humble, by worth of character and disinterested exertion, promotes, in ways the most effectual, its prosperity and efficiency. Pecuniarily the largest, and by his example among the best, of its benefactors, is Joshua Fisher, eminent as a physician and civilian, a president of the Massachusetts Medical Society, State senator, founder of the leading charitable institution of this town, which is named after him, and of the professorship of Natural History in Harvard University, also bearing his name: withal, throughout a very long life, taking a large and liberal interest in all subjects, — religious, political, social, or of any kind that related to the good of individuals and society. Connected with him in establishing, during the earlier part of my ministry, a parochial fund, was Israel Thorndike, — who, born here in obscurity, illustrated in his course the equal right of all our people to aspire and strive for the highest positions of affluence or power; having, from small beginnings, become a merchant-prince, and accumulated at his decease one of the largest fortunes then possessed in New England. His great abilities, manifested in public and private spheres, were extensively known and freely admitted. While his memory will be perpetuated in the University by his rare and valuable gift of the Ebeling Library, it will also be cherished as that of a generous supporter and friend of this his native parish.

Following the second pastor were three in succession bearing the christened name Joseph, on whom the mantle — of wisdom, prudence, purity, and fidelity to all relations — of the son of Jacob seems to have fallen. The first was Joseph Champney, whose ministry is the longest as yet in this parish, having been protracted to its forty-fourth year. Mild and retiring in his disposition, he did not attain marked prominence of reputation and influence. But being affectionate, earnest, devoted to the welfare of his people, a warm, mutual regard and attachment from the first sprang up between him and them, which lasted and strengthened through their long connection, and followed him to his grave. If deficient to a degree in energy of character, he had in Robert Hale, the grandson of the first minister, and his own college classmate and friend, a strong right arm, a veritable tower of strength, on which to lean amid all his parochial duties and responsibilities, who was at his side, a powerful lay colleague, from the beginning to almost the close of his long ministry. Rarely, here or anywhere, has arisen the man, who, more than Hale, has left a deep, broad mark of versatile ability on the community in which, from birth to death, he lived. His precocity is sufficiently evinced by the fact, that, in his sixteenth year, he was appointed master of the grammar school of the town. "Facile princeps," meaning natural and ready leader, would seem to have been written on his forehead at his very birth. It is positively bewildering to run through the list of the various and multiplied offices — professional (for he was bred a physician), civil, military, ecclesiastical — which he discharged; yet with an unfailing, never-faltering method, sagacity, and efficiency. Whether engaged in municipal offices, or in superintending the schools and watching over the interests of education, or in the concerns of the church and parish, or in those of the county of which for some time he was high sheriff, or in military affairs (having had command of a regiment, and taken a leading part under Pepperell in the siege and reduction of Louisbourg), or in financial matters, or in business of the province (having served many years as a member of the legislature and of the governor's council, or in important negotiations intrusted to him between this and other provinces), — in all he was alike eminent and influential. So that when he drew up the rules for seating the congregation, already quoted, and the otherwise delicate duty devolved on him of providing the uppermost seat for himself, such was the general deference to his character and position as to free him from embarrassment in so doing. There were none to question or dispute his full right and title to the first place, either under that or any previous code framed for the same purpose.

For several of the later years of Mr. Champney's pastorate, the subject was much agitated of replacing the second meeting-house with a third. At length the work was commenced and pursued in good earnest. The temple — which had stood on this spot and spread its sheltering wings over three generations of worshippers, and been to many, we trust, the house of God and gate of heaven — was taken down, and this in which we are now gathered was erected in its stead; public worship, meanwhile, being conducted under a large tree near the pastor's residence, at the easterly end of the common. This house, at the beginning, was decidedly in advance of its predecessor, in appearance and accommodations. Still, it was not without its drawbacks; among which may be mentioned, deficiency in arrangements for warming: and the seats being on hinges, from which, at the rising and sitting of the assembly, proceeded a sound which has been fitly compared to the rattling produced by a running fire of musketry. Owing to the growth of the parish, it was materially enlarged in a quarter of a century from its erection, and so continued till, forty years later, it was thoroughly repaired, remodelled, furnished with a new organ, and beautifully frescoed; so that the text I chose for the re-opening was scarcely extravagant for its description, — "The workmen wrought, and the work was perfected by them; and they set the house of God in its state, and strengthened it." But thirty years and more have since glided away, — glided past not a few of us. New, and in some respects undoubtedly better, tastes have arisen and been nurtured. In accordance with them, the house that was builded many years ago has been builded again. The place of the sanctuary has been at once beautified and rendered more commodious. The walls from which echoed the tones of the solemn, earnest, devout voices of four of your deceased and revered pastors, stand in pristine strength, in renovated freshness, and added beauty; ready, we hope, to receive and welcome all who shall be gathered within them to better impulses, more favoring and benign auspices, a more improved moral and spiritual condition, than have before been here known and enjoyed. When I learned, that, in the recent alterations, the old oaken frame was found undecayed, rather hardened and made firm by age, I was reminded of an eccentric minister, who, on being consulted by a committee of his society as to the expediency of repairing or building anew their church, instantly replied, "By all means repair, for I can vouch for the soundness of the sleepers." I beg you, my friends, not to suppose for a moment that the covert but thinly-veiled satire thus conveyed is intended in the least for you. If so, I should fear being met by the query, "Who was it that put us to sleep?" Be assured, I have experienced too much and long your patience and wakeful attention, in listening to my humble utterances, to apprehend in the slightest degree any occasion for reviving among you an early New-England practice, the description of which I give in the words of the annalist, —

"In some places it was customary, during the public service, for a person to go about the meeting-house to wake the sleepers. He bore a long wand, on one end of which was a ball, and on the other a fox-tail. When he observed the men asleep, he rapped them on the head with the knob; and roused the slumbering sensibilities of the ladies by drawing the brush slightly across their faces."

A few months before Mr. Champney's death, in 1773, Joseph Willard was settled as colleague-pastor. Coming as he did from the college at Cambridge, where he had passed ten previous years as pupil and tutor, with a high reputation as a scholar, theologian, and man, he was welcomed cordially by the majority of the parish. Some there were who were troubled with doubts about the soundness of his faith; the Arminian controversy being then rife, and he being suspected, not without reason, of having proclivities in that direction. All opposition, however, was soon disarmed by his prudence, his weight of character, his devotedness to the ministerial office and pastoral duty, and, I may add, by his good-humored treatment of the easily-disturbed and alarmed. To one not conversant with theological terms, who said to him, "They do say that you are a musk-melon," — that being the questioner's nearest approach to the name Arminian, — he smilingly answered, "Don't you believe it; for, if I had been, I should long ere this have been eaten up." However, he soon was firmly and universally fixed in the confidence and affections of his people, and ever afterward so continued. His ministry here was cast in troublous and trying times. The seeds of the Revolution, that was to separate this from the mother country, had been sown and were fast germinating. A true patriot himself, he contributed much to kindle and keep alive the general flame of patriotism. And not in word only, but in deeds, was his patriotic devotion shown. On the ever-memorable 19th of April, 1775, when alarm-bells and guns were sounded, and messengers were riding with hot haste in every direction to announce that the war had begun, and rouse the populations to arms, he was among the first to repair to the scene of bloody conflict; and it is a fact worthy of note, to be ascribed in no small part to his exertions and influence, that two companies from this town bore a part in the fight, having one of their men killed and several wounded, and having marched a greater distance than had any others engaged in the contest.

He also took an intelligent and active interest in civil affairs. His fellow-townsmen often availed themselves of the aid of his sound judgment, his practical wisdom, and energy. For instance, I find his name on a committee to report on a constitution for the State, which was rejected; and again, two years later, in 1780, on the one then framed and adopted. He was constantly in consultation with leading citizens, and frequently joined with them on committees for public business. Upon both of those just named, he was connected with his confidential friend and parishioner, George Cabot, — who was then developing the character for business capacity and action, for surpassing conversational talent and address, for political sagacity, — as a civilian, a man, and a Christian, — which carried with it a charmed spell and power over men's minds in the wide circle within which he moved, enabled him to attain marked distinction in the State and national councils, and gave him a prominent rank among the distinguished and able men of the country. There were other objects, outside of his professional avocations, that claimed and shared Mr. Willard's attention and exertions. Deeply interested and ever watchful for the right and thorough training of the young, he was indifferent to none of the means by which those of an older growth might have their minds enlarged and cultivated. At the same time, he was not unmindful of, but looked well to, the discipline and expansion of his own intellect. Indeed, considering the engrossing nature of his profession, which was so sustained by him as — instead of his being subject to the imputation of neglecting its duties — to make him regarded, in and out of the parish, a pattern of devotedness to their fulfilment, it is amazing that he should have accomplished what he did in other departments. Amid the pressure of parochial cares and professional engagements, and notwithstanding the excitements, privations, and struggles of the Revolutionary war, that raged through the larger part of his ministry, and in which he acted and endured a no inconsiderable part, he never remitted his habits of application to literature and science. In the classics, particularly the Greek, he was an eminent scholar; which is the more remarkable, from the circumstance of his not having commenced the study of the ancient languages till after he was of age. Mathematics, astronomy, and natural philosophy were also favorite studies with him; in the pursuit of the last two, having procured and been aided by a set of valuable instruments. On the dark day of May, 1780, — supposed to have been caused by dense clouds of smoke from a distance, which in a peculiar state of the atmosphere hovered over this region, — when the light of mid-day was suddenly

8

changed to the darkness of night, and fear and trepidation
seized upon the animal creation, scarcely less than man, Mr.
Willard, like the true philosopher he was, took a station on the
green in front of his house, with the requisite apparatus, to
examine and interpret, if possible, the solemnly impressive phe-
nomena. Soon numbers of persons gathered around him in a
state of intense alarm and terror, whom his calmness and self-
possession, and wise and kind words, did much to tranquillize
and re-assure. As he was proceeding with his observations, a
man nearly out of breath rushed up to him with the announce-
ment, " The tide has done flowing ; " when, quietly looking at
his watch, he deliberately replied, " So it has, for it is just high-
water." In 1781, one of the numerous privateers from this
quarter — that did so much, by their depredations on British
commerce, to reconcile Britain to the loss of " the brightest jewel
of her crown," and bring the war of the Revolution to a close —
arrived at this port, under command of the noted Hugh Hill,
with a prize captured on the English coast. It was owned by
Andrew Cabot and John his brother, — two intelligent, enter-
prising, and public-spirited citizens of the town, opulent mer-
chants, — whose expensive, spacious, and imposing mansions,
striking in appearance as they now stand, must have been much
more so in the comparative simplicity of the period in which
they were reared ; and from whose families that peerless trio
of brothers, Charles, James, and Patrick T. Jackson, so eminent
and worthy in their respective walks of life (the legal, medical,
and mercantile), obtained their excellent wives. Among the
treasures contained in the prize, and, as it proved, far the most
valuable of them all, was the celebrated Kirwan library, consisting of more than a hundred scientific works, ancient and modern,
which, when taken, was in transit from England to its proprietor
in Ireland. At the suggestion of Mr. Willard, the owners
generously relinquished their title to it ; allowing it to be sold, in
compliance with law, to an association of gentlemen resident
here and in Salem, for a mere nominal price, — the sum of
thirty-eight shillings actually paid for it being out of all proportion and ludicrously small, compared with its intrinsic value and

beneficial results. To the honor of Richard Kirwan, it should be mentioned, that he declined an offer of compensation for his property in it, preferring to have it pass for an outright gift to the infant cause and scanty means of scientific progress, in a country not yet emerged from the clouds of desperate strife with his own for separate national existence; and this is the more honorable to him, for the magnanimous superiority he thus showed to the jealousies and enmities inevitably growing out of war. The books, so fortunately secured, were first committed to Willard's keeping, in the assurance, no doubt, that in his hands they would be well cared for and faithfully used and improved, — under certain rules, nevertheless, for the free use of them by any members of the association to which they belonged. Upon his removal from Beverly they were transferred to Salem, where they were united with other collections, first under the name of the Philosophical Library, then that of the Salem Athenæum, and finally of the Essex Institute, of which flourishing, richly endowed, greatly valued and useful institution it may be considered a, if not the, germ. From that germ alone great advantage has by not a few been derived. Our famous mathematician, Nathaniel Bowditch, of world-wide fame, availed himself extensively of the aid afforded by the Kirwan books, especially in the earlier portion of his remarkable career, when such works were rare and difficult, at least in this country, to be procured; and his sense of indebtedness, for the valuable assistance he derived from them, was freely and gratefully acknowledged by him while living, and testified at his decease by a liberal legacy to the institution in which they are deposited, and of which they form a part.

Just as Mr. Willard was about entering on the tenth year of his pastorate, he was elected by a unanimous vote of the overseers of Harvard College to its presidency. Honorable as was the appointment, it was very far from being a position of ease or irresponsibility to which he was invited. Any one reading Quincy's history of the institution will perceive at a glance that it was to no bed of roses, or dignified leisure, to which he was called. The Revolutionary war was raging. Demoraliza-

tion, connected with and resulting from it, had not passed the
college by. Discipline and education in it, the habits of study
and morals of the students, had not escaped the disturbing and
deteriorating influences that were abroad. Financial embarrass-
ments, threatening absolute failure, pressed heavily on all engaged in its government, on all imparting or receiving instruction.
Besides, the presidential office had been vacant for more than a
year, and during the preceding six years had been occupied by
one who, with acknowledged learning and virtues, was deficient
in the qualities requisite for its successful administration. But
Willard was not to be deterred by obstacles, however formidable,
in the way whither duty pointed. After mature and "prayerful
consideration, weighing things on every side, and consulting the
most judicious persons," he decided to enter on the task which
he felt Providence had assigned him. With this view, he re-
quested of the parish a dismissal from his pastoral relation to it,
which, though with extreme reluctance, was granted; and in
December, 1781, he took public and affecting leave of his
charge.

In the new and wider sphere on which he at once entered,
he soon proved himself the right man in the right place. His
executive abilities were of a high order, which — I have the
authority of the late Judge White, who was his pupil, and subsequently his associate in the college faculty, for saying — fitted
him to fill even a wider sphere of duty than any to which he was
called. The gentleman just alluded to, whom so many of us
have been accustomed to respect and love, relates, in illustrating
his readiness of resource and decision of character, that when,
in the chapel, before an assembly of the officers and students, he
had sentenced one of the latter to a punishment not the sever-
est, who immediately broke out into language most disrespectful
and rebellious, he calmly summoned the members of the government present around him, and, after a few moments' consultation, with equal calmness subjected the offender to the highest
collegiate penalty, — that of expulsion. His administration, like
his character, had prominent features, and also traits in striking
contrast with each other. Behind a veil of strict reserve were a

vein of humor and wit, and a keen relish for them. Dignified in aspect, at times almost stern, he was mild and benignant in spirit. Formal in manner, he was tender and loving at heart. Under a sway affectionate, and parental even, he exerted steadily the magnetism of a strong will. "Having been called," says Quincy, "to the president's chair in the midst of the Revolutionary war, when the general tone of morals was weak and the spirit of discipline enervated, he sustained the authority of his station with consummate steadfastness and prudence. He found the seminary embarrassed; he left it free and prosperous. His influence was uniformly happy, and, throughout his whole connection with the institution, he enjoyed the entire confidence of his associates in the government, the respect of the students, and the undeviating approbation and support of the public."

His death — which occurred in September, 1804, after some years of failing health, and which closed the longest term of service but one in the series of Harvard's Presidents, that of nearly twenty-three years — was the signal for wide-spread lamentation and profound regrets. But nowhere was the event more sincerely and deeply mourned, nowhere up to this day is he more reverently and gratefully remembered, than in this scene of his first and only ministry. Since the termination of that ministry, more than fourscore years have passed away; but memorials are not wanting to keep fresh and fragrant among us the recollection of him who fulfilled it. The venerable mansion, still standing, in which he lived, in which centred his domestic joys and laborious studies; the beautiful green before it, where he exercised at once body and mind, where he observed the courses of nature, watched the stars, their relative positions, the motions of the heavenly bodies whose orbits he delighted to follow and calculate; these streets he daily walked, these dwellings in which he was greeted as pastor and friend, this temple at whose altar he ministered in holy things; this Bible now before me, which, rising superior to the narrow and anti-Episcopalian prejudices that had previously prevailed in this church and the Puritan churches generally, he caused to be procured for the public reading of the Scriptures in divine service, and from which the lively and sacred oracles have for nearly a century been uttered in the hearing of the people here worshipping; moreover, and best, the influence he exerted on those to whom he ministered, which has not ceased, and will not cease to be transmitted to their successors, — all these are present and living remembrancers of him, and through them, though a long time dead, he yet is with us.

An interval of over three years occurred between the retirement of President Willard and the settlement of his successor, — produced perhaps partly by fastidiousness of taste, partly by differing predilections for individuals among the numerous candidates employed and heard, partly also by growing diversities of theological sentiment, and probably in no small part from the unsettled state of affairs springing out of the war, and the consequences immediately following it. At length the choice fell on Joseph McKean, whom any religious society would have been fortunate in choosing and securing for its pastoral office, which having accepted he was ordained in May, 1785, — his honored predecessor preaching the ordination sermon from the text, "For God hath not given us the spirit of fear, but of power, and of love, and of a sound mind." And no words could have better delineated the chief elements in the character of both. Of McKean might it truly be said, that he had the sound mind in a sound body. He had what I esteem a decided advantage, — to have been brought up under the influences of country life. "From his early youth he was strong and athletic, able to support fatigue and endure hardship; and in his youth, and long after, excelled in all the manly exercises to which the active and hardy yeomanry of our country were then accustomed." A noted wrestler once, and as the experiment proved in all probability never again, called on him to test their relative strength and skill. The challenger was promptly conducted to a retired spot on the premises; and the suddenness with which he was reduced from an erect to a reclining posture convinced him that the minister of this parish was not less competent to wrestle with flesh and blood, than with spiritual wickedness. His talents were solid, rather than brilliant, — discriminating judgment being a marked quality of his mind. Beyond his professional avocations, in which he was well informed, diligent, and faithful, the exact sciences were favorite objects of his pursuit. Contributions on these were made by him to the Transactions of the American Academy, — which, together with a few occasional sermons, and the inaugural address at Brunswick, are his only publications. Of his printed discourses is one, which was delivered under peculiar circumstances, and produced an extensive and strong impression. Its subject is, "Speaking Evil of Rulers." It was preached soon after Jefferson's accession to the Presidency, to an assembly, the mass of which, including the preacher himself, was strenuously opposed to the new administration. It reproved calmly, but firmly and unsparingly, the lax and violent speech toward the powers that be, then prevalent and too common at all times. Yet so mildly, so judiciously and effectively, was the rebuke conveyed, that, when heard, or widely as it was perused, it was generally acknowledged to be just and wholesome ; and, as we read it now, must be admitted not merely to have been specially adapted to that emergency, but to be of universal application. Mr. McKean was, in truth, remarkably sagacious in discerning the characters of men, and equally wise and skilful in dealing with them. Thus was he peculiarly fitted to guide and control the young men gathered in a seminary of learning such as that over which he was ultimately called to preside. Altogether, he possessed, by nature and acquired excellence, a combination of gifts, which singularly qualified him for exerting a positive and extended influence. Imposing in stature and bearing, earnest in whatever he undertook, always frank, generous, and magnanimous, never compromising the dignity and decorum becoming a minister and a gentleman, condescending and tender to the humble and lowest, the courteous and recognized peer of the most refined and exalted in rank or station, he secured to an uncommon degree the respect, affection, and confidence of all with whom he came in contact, alike high and low, rich and poor, and of whatever condition. His advice was sought and relied on by persons of every class, in matters secular and civil, as well as pertaining directly to his profession. He took an intelligent and active interest in the grand and stirring political events that were passing before him. The record of his name and co-operation stands conspicuous by the side of that of eminent leaders in important affairs of the town, the State, and nation. Nor was he more ready to impart of his wise counsel, than when occasion required to labor with his strong arms and hands. Thus, when the great cable for the now nobly historic frigate "Constitution" was in preparation here, and its speedy completion was very desirable, he volunteered his valuable assistance in its manufacture; so, and variously otherwise, manifesting his own patriotic enthusiasm and devotion, and by his example kindling and keeping alive a corresponding flame in others' breasts. Possessing such characteristics as have been just described, he could hardly fail to be honored, influential, and beloved among his parishioners, his fellow-townsmen, and in the community wherever known. They eminently fitted him to be useful, acceptable, and ever-welcome, in performing the more retired duties of the pastoral office. In the pulpit he was solemn, devout, instructive, sustained, and impressive. His sermons were plain and practical, — intended not for display of learning or sensational effect, but to do good, to awaken and deepen moral and religious impressions, — yet often composed with careful elaboration. Having been born and brought up among the Scotch-Irish Presbyterians, who settled in Londonderry, New Hampshire, he had received and retained a tinge of Calvinistic associations, of which he may never have been rid. But he was far from obtruding them on the notice of his hearers; and dwelt, and in public and private delighted to dwell, on the main fundamental principles and precepts of Christianity, that reach far down beyond any mere dogmas of man's invention or discovery. That he was no more than what was termed a moderate Calvinist, is evidenced by the fact, that toward the close of his ministry measures were adopted for forming out of this a new society, — not on account of the overgrown state of the parish, which then in all probability was the largest in New England, numbering little if any less than three thousand souls; but ostensibly and avowedly because a sufficiently rigid standard of orthodoxy was not upheld in it, and by its minister. He was indeed thoroughly and truly a liberal Christian, claiming for himself the unrestricted right to prove all things, to hold and utter what he believed to be true and good, and conceding to all men of all minds an equal right and title.

After seventeen years' devoted service and usefulness here, with lasting mutual regrets, and friendships more enduring, he relinquished his pastoral relation, and assumed the duties, and trials too, of first President of Bowdoin College; a position to which he was urgently called, for which his character and abilities peculiarly qualified him, and where they found ample scope for exercise. On this new sphere he entered with alacrity, and in the five short years allotted to him he accomplished much. Though summoned from earth in the midst of his days, being only in his fiftieth year when the summons came, he left behind him a rising and prosperous institution of learning, based on broad and secure foundations; and now the taper he lighted upon it has become a burning and shining light in the East.

The ministry last sketched fell, as I have intimated, on troubled times. True, there was no open and declared war, — always to be reckoned among the direst of evils and calamities. But there were heavy debts accumulated during the Revolution, onerous taxes consequent thereon, a currency depreciated almost to no value at all, commerce and business stagnant or in stark derangement; rebellion, even in staid Massachusetts, against the constituted authorities; the confederation of States felt to be, what it has been aptly compared to, a rope of sand; the framing and adoption of the Federal constitution of government; the administrations of Washington, and the elder Adams, and the incoming of Jefferson's; interspersed with agitating questions and party conflicts at home, with threatening wars and jeopardized independence from abroad. All these difficulties and exigencies were met by members of this parish in a manner alike able and noteworthy.

Without enumerating in detail the services thus rendered, I

9

must be permitted to detain you for a few moments, in remarking the striking part performed by some of your own number, and another intimately connected with you, in the most momentous issue ever presented to this nation ; being nothing less than the existence and indefinite extension of negro slavery in our land, or its total extirpation from it. To the lot of Nathan Dane, for more than a half century a consistent and devout member of this society, it fell, or rather he wisely and bravely assumed the responsibility, of taking the great initiatory step toward banishing that plague-spot on the body politic, that dark stain on our country's escutcheon, that foul disgrace and burning shame of our republican institutions. A native of the county town of Ipswich, a graduate with high distinction at Harvard, he commenced and pursued through a prolonged life the profession of his choice ; earning, by his diligence and abilities, the title — pronounced upon him by no less an authority than Judge Story — of Father of American Law, and, by his reputation and liberal endowments, leaving his name to designate the law school of the university in which he was trained, and to which, through a long life, he was warmly attached. Above all did he honor himself and dignify his profession, by being true, honest, just, and worthy, as a lawyer, not less than as a man and Christian. Instead of fostering litigation, as self-interest and professional bias might have seemed to prompt, he habitually and from principle discouraged it ; thus carrying out in spirit, and all the more effectively from the motives which would naturally have been supposed to lead him to a contrary course, the spirit of the rule adopted in the first Boston church within five years from its formation, that none shall sue till certain persons named " have had the hearing and deciding of the case, if they can." To his honorable and disinterested conduct in this regard have been ascribed, by those with the best opportunities of observing and judging it, the peculiar aversion to litigiousness, and comparatively rare cases of contestants at court, among the population with which, as legal adviser and practitioner, he was more immediately connected. A man with character founded on such a basis, was not slow in being called by the suffrages of an intelligent and patriotic constituency to public service, to assist in framing the laws he was so fitted to expound and apply. In 1785, he was elected to the State legislature, in which he performed valuable service; at least, this may be inferred from his being commissioned, the following year, a member of the old Congress. Scarcely had he taken his seat, when he was advanced to a commanding position in that body. In the year 1787, — that year ever memorable in the history of our country and his own fame, — he, as chairman of a committee, reported resolves for assembling at Philadelphia (that name symbolical of national as well as brotherly union) the convention that framed the Constitution of the United States; and that same year he drafted and carried to its final passage the ordinance by which slavery was for ever banished from, and freedom secured to, the whole vast territory north-west of the Ohio River. Mingled with his various and engrossing occupations as a lawyer and statesman, together with necessary attention to his private affairs, were historical and theological investigations, for both of which he had a decided taste. The immense amount he accomplished, as a public man, a student, writer, and author, can be accounted for only by marvellous industry, combined with uncommon mental and physical powers. Through his long and laborious life, he was blessed with the sympathy, counsel, and active co-operation of a wife whom, though childless, many of us remember as truly a mother in Israel; to whom, departing at a very advanced age, was specially due the scriptural eulogium, "She hath done what she could." She accompanied him, while a member of Congress, during some of its sessions. Often has it been my privilege to listen to vivid descriptions, by that venerable couple, of scenes of absorbing interest, witnessed by them at the seat of government, in the closing years of the old Confederation, and under the administration of Washington.

But the singular felicity, the rare opportunity well and gloriously improved, which the genius of our civil history will assign to Mr. Dane, consist in his having been the author of the Ordinance of '87, for the government of the North-western Territory. " We are accustomed," said Daniel Webster, in the

Senate, " to praise the lawgivers of antiquity ; we help to per-
petuate the fame of Solon and Lycurgus : but I doubt whether
one single law of any lawgiver, ancient or modern, has produced
effects of more distinct, marked, and lasting character than the
Ordinance of 1787." Its prohibition of involuntary servitude,
resting on original compact, reaching deeper down than all local
laws or constitutions, stamped on the virgin soil the enduring
imprint of freedom, and barred it for ever from being trod by
the feet of slaves. Where, I cannot but here ask, should we
have been, where would our nation be now, if this seasonable
provision had not been made ? How different, probably, would
have been the result of the late tremendous civil war, had the
great North-west been originally given over to slavery, and been
in alliance with the slave power, instead of sending forth from
her teeming millions hosts of brave men to fight the battles of
liberty, — her world-renowned generals, moreover, to conduct
our armies to victorious triumph.

Nathan Dane's is not the only voice from among you that has
made itself heard and felt in the halls of Congress on this
momentous subject. More than threescore years had passed,
during which the evil, that the Ordinance was specially designed
to forefend, grew steadily in magnitude and force ; became an
object of serious alarm and conscientious horror to multitudes of
true patriots, of devout and Christian men and women ; caused
Jefferson, from the midst of a slaveholding community, to exclaim, " I tremble for my country, when I remember that God
is just ; " had raised an agitation which was no ghost to " down
at the bidding " of any man or body of men, but which, the more
loudly and fiercely it was denounced, would be the more deter-
minedly carried on, as relating to a mighty wrong, in the awful
consequences of which not slaves only, but the whole people,
shared, and for which a responsibility, moral, if not civil, — and
by not a few taken in both lights, — was widely and intensely
felt. It was felt to be, and was, a canker at the root, a cancer
at the vitals, which had sent a subtle and deleterious influence
through the veins and arteries, and was eating into the heart, of
the nation. Yet it had its apologists, advocates, and supporters,

with a controlling agency at the seat of the national government, demanding its recognition as a general rather than sectional interest, — not only that the law for return of fugitive slaves should be rigidly executed in all the States, slave and free alike, but that masters should be at liberty to take their slaves into any part of the country, and in the territories especially bring slavery into direct and full competition with freedom. Moreover, there were not wanting those, and they were not few, who were ready to denounce and stigmatize with base aspersions, and visit with ostracism, any who boldly stood up for human rights and civil liberty against such monstrous and outrageous assumptions. Personal safety was often risked and seriously endangered in the case of standard-bearers in freedom's cause. Threats of life-peril were breathed against them, which were not always empty or unexecuted.

It was in this juncture of political affairs, in this posture of our national concerns and interests, that Robert Rantoul, Jr., entered on his duties as a member of Congress. He had sometime before volunteered, amid severe reproach, not to say obloquy, and in spite of the prevailing sentiment, in the defence of a fugitive slave, whose rendition was claimed under the operation of the Fugitive-slave Law. That law he maintained was unconstitutional, and therefore by due legal process to be set aside and rendered inoperative. Whatever may be the conclusions at which different minds might arrive on the point, it must be admitted that it was discussed by him with consummate ability. On that occasion he was associated with, and nobly sustained by, another of your attached and highly esteemed fellow-parishioners, Charles G. Loring, — whose presence, prevented by extreme illness, we sadly miss to-day, — whose pen, tongue, and purse, and talents and weight of character, have ever been forward to enlist in every good cause, and through our late public trials have rendered service of incalculable benefit. Mr. Rantoul's position having been thus clearly defined and well understood, he was early called on, after taking his seat in Congress, to defend that position. This he did with a frankness and power which, while delighting his friends, commanded the unfeigned respect and deference, admiration even, of his bitterest opponents. Listen to these earnest, searching, viewed in the light of recent events almost prophetic, utterances, which experience has proved wise and true, as they were brave, at the time they were delivered : —

" Do the Southern gentlemen know what they are doing? Do they mean to throw the whole power over the subject of slavery into the hands of the Federal Government? You do it here. Do gentlemen desire that two-thirds of the white men of the country, aye, a great. many more than two-thirds very soon, . . . should take the subject of slavery into their hands, — to let it agitate, and agitate, and convulse the whole nation, until it shall finally be treated as it will be treated, if it becomes the fuel of a universal conflagration through this land. Let Southern gentlemen take warning in this matter. . . . It may result in civil war and anarchy. I say that is possible ; but in my opinion it is a mere possibility. But it is a possibility that prudent men ought to look at, because bad management may drive the chariot off the precipice, when, with the slightest degree of prudence and skill, the course would be perfectly safe. It may result in civil war, if badly managed indeed, without any sort of prudence. . . . Slavery will not last for ever, for the seeds of its death are within itself. Now almost the whole civilized world have got rid of it ; and that portion of the civilized world which still retains this institution, retains a temporary institution, and it must look about to see how, with the least inconvenience and suffering to itself, that temporary institution is to come to an end. That is the great question for Southern men ; and if it is to be pressed upon this government, — and I think it ought not to be, — then it is the great question for Northern men. . . . Agitation is not to be quieted by hard words. Hard words will have very little success on either side. This question of slavery can be quieted only in two ways. One way will be for the South to let it alone ; and then, if everybody at the North would let it alone, which no man can promise, it would be quieted. The other would be, to talk about it like reasonable men. Take it up as you take up any other great national interest, and try to get at the merits of it. When you do that, it will be then as quietly approached and treated as any other subject ; and, by the blessing of Providence on your honest endeavors, a way will be found to pass through that transition of social system through which most of the nations of Europe have passed within a comparatively recent period."

When he who thus spoke had been stricken down by fatal disease, in the meridian of his powers and the full tide of their successful exertion, and the lips from which such eloquent and forcible words proceeded were sealed in the silence of death, his successor, Charles W. Upham, did not hesitate to take up the gauntlet he had so courageously accepted and ably met, but which had fallen from his lifeless hand, and did battle with similar ability, courage, and sagacious foresight on the great, exciting topic; which, though coming up under some variation of form, was still the same in substance, and in the intent and purpose for which the controversy was raised. It is very observable, that the two representatives of this district, belonging (I may on this occasion add) to this and the mother parish, should have coincided to the extent they did in the sentiments they held and uttered at that period, and in the distinguished part they bore in the war of words and ideas which preceded the impending conflict of arms. In the debate of 1854 in Congress, on the Kansas and Nebraska bill, Mr. Upham said (and what has occurred since gives deep significance to the language then used) : —

"I hold that this bill contemplates, and will if it becomes a law constitute, a radical and vital change in the policy on which the union of these States was originally formed, and by which its affairs have been administered throughout its entire history. It will be an abandonment of the course that has been pursued from the first. The country will swing from her moorings, and we shall embark, with all the precious interests, all the glorious recollections, and all the magnificent prospects of this vast republican empire, upon an untraversed, unknown, and it may well be feared stormy, if not fatal, sea. Heretofore the South has profited by our divisions. Those divisions have arisen, to a great degree, from the restraining and embarrassing influence of a sense of obligation on our part to adhere to the engagements and stand up to the bargains made by the fathers, and renewed, as I have shown, by each succeeding generation. But let those engagements be violated; let those bargains be broken by the South, on the ground of unconstitutionality, or any other pretence, — from that hour the North becomes a unit and indivisible; from that hour 'Northern men with Southern principles' will disappear from the scene, and the race of dough-faces be extinct for ever. I do not threaten. I pretend to no gift of prophecy. Any man can interpret the gathering signs of the times. All can read the handwriting on the wall. The very intimation that the Missouri Compromise is proposed to be repealed by Southern votes, in defiance of the protest of four-fifths of the Northern representatives, has rallied the people of the free States as they have never been rallied before. Their simultaneous and indignant protests pour in upon your table, in petitions, resolutions, and remonstrances, without number and without end. They are repeated in popular assemblages, from the seashore to the Rocky Mountains; and in the newspaper press of all parties, and all creeds, and all languages. You have united the free States at last, by this untimely, unprovoked, and astounding proposal. If you execute it by the passage of this bill, they wil lbe united for ever in one unbroken, universal, and uncompromising resistance of the encroachments of the slave-power everywhere and at all points, whether north or south of 36° 30'. Their unalterable determination is heard over the whole breadth of the land, proclaiming, in thunder tones, What has been pledged to freedom shall be free for ever.

"If you pass the bill, or if it is defeated in spite of the combined Southern vote, there will be an end of all compromises. Some of them may remain in the letter of the Constitution, but it will be a dead letter; their moral force will be gone for ever. The honorable member from South Carolina intimated that perhaps it would be well to abandon the policy of compromises, and for the two great conflicting interests to meet face to face, and end the matter at once. I have suggested the reasons why, heretofore, I have contemplated such an issue with reluctance. But if the South say so, so let it be."

But I have trespassed too long on your patient listening, and must hasten to gather and present the events and thoughts which could not properly be omitted on the present occasion. They fall chiefly within the compass of the passing century. The ministry of Abiel Abbot commenced in 1803. I hardly need sketch, or attempt to sketch it, — so familiar is it to many of you, fathers and mothers, who have told it from your personal experience, better far than by me it could be described

or narrated, to your children. Born and bred under Christian
influences, with a heart to receive and improve them, he may be
said to have been a minister of religion from and by birth ; even
as the poet proverbially is born, not made, — *nascitur, non fit.*
His ministerial course here, as I have learned more and more
of it, has seemed to me to picture an all but Elysian pastor's
life. With the delights of an intellectual, refined, religious,
and happy home ; a parish composed of great varieties in
culture and social condition, with all which he had the good
sense and right feeling to be in cordial sympathy ; with ready
and unfailing tact to adapt himself to all conditions and circumstances, " his whole manner so informed with the grace of a
kindly and persuasive wisdom ; " in his own or other pulpits
always acceptable and welcome ; an acknowledged light, guide,
and ornament of society ; regarded among his parishioners,
townsmen, and the community the friend and pillar of learning, virtue, and religion, — how could his position be otherwise
than most desirable, and, if envy might be supposed to intrude,
be more enviable ? An instance of his readiness of resource at
this moment occurs to me. When called to preach in a neighboring parish, where one of those unfortunate jars, which will
sometimes occur in the best-regulated choirs, had happened, he
found the singers' seats wholly vacated. After reading the
hymn, he announced the tune, invited the congregation to join
him in it, and led off in the singing, followed by such numbers and
with such effect, that the choir, if only for fear that their occu-
pation would be gone, concluded to return, change their discord
to harmony, and take their usual part in the afternoon service.
In Sprague's " Annals of the American Pulpit," that monument
of industry, of talented and liberal research, it is mentioned by
the author himself, that he was witness of the effort made by
Abbot when the Consociation of Connecticut had his brother
on trial and decided on deposing him ; and pronounces his management of the case and final argument to rank among the
best instances of knowledge of ecclesiastical law, and ability
in its illustration and enforcement. No man could be, more
sincerely and earnestly than he was, a lover of peace. Yet

commotions, disturbing causes, and contests, neither few nor small, were embraced within the time of his ministry. During a portion of it, there was bitter strife between political parties: there was the embargo under Jefferson's, and the war with Great Britain under Madison's, Administration, — both of which bore very heavily on this commercial and seafaring population. Controversy on religious topics also broke out, and was pursued with great warmth and vigor, not to say violence. It arose naturally, inevitably, from radical differences of opinion among those whom we are bound to believe equally sincere and earnest followers of Christ and of God. If he of whom I am speaking, amid the din of theological disputation, were of the number who strove to hush it, and cried peace when there was no peace, it must be attributed in no small part to his peace-loving spirit, and furthermore to a circumstance by no means to be left out of the account, — that a respectable minority of his parish, between whom and himself there existed strong personal regard and attachment, differed from the great majority and from him, by being Trinitarian and Calvinistic.

Above all was he a lover of the profession which, together with its objects, he had from his youth espoused, — which he adorned, in the discharge of the duties of which he delighted, and to which he gave his best energies. When, in the midst of his labors and usefulness, he was arrested by disease, and admonished to seek the restoring influence of a milder clime, among his last words before quitting — as the event proved for ever — his dearly loved home, were these, uttered to an intimate professional friend: "I believe the hour of my departure is at hand, — how near I cannot say; but not far distant is the time when I shall be in the immediate presence of my Maker. This impression leads me to look back upon my life, and inwardly upon my present state. In the review, I find many things to be humble and penitent for, and many things to fill me with gratitude and praise. I have, I trust, the testimony of my heart, that my life, my best powers, my time, and my efforts have, in the main, been sincerely given to God and mankind." His publications consist of two volumes of sermons, a catechism, several occasional discourses, and a posthumous volume of letters from Cuba; which last, written under failing health, addressed to the endeared members of his family household, pervaded by love and correct appreciation of the beautiful and true in nature or human character, showing careful observation and nice discrimination between the good and bad, and devout recognition, throughout, of the God over all and in all, — so altogether genial, affectionate, pious, and delectable, that it has struck me, as I doubt not it has some of you, — like the notes attributed to the dying swan, — as among the sweetest and best of his productions.

It was during his pastorship that the first Sunday school, as that institution now exists and is conducted, was founded in connection with this parish. This was in 1810, nearly sixty years ago. Two young ladies, Misses Prince and Hill, commenced the good work by collecting, on the sabbath, poor and neglected children, to whom they imparted religious instruction, and whom at least they hoped and helped to rescue from temptation and harm. In this good enterprise they received the cordial co-operation of the pastor and other influential friends. So interesting and attractive did they make it, and so popular did it quickly become, that the more, not less than the least, favored children and youths gladly came forward to partake of its benefits; and it soon grew to be an adopted and favorite foster-child of the parish. Within a few years, the example thus afforded was copied into neighboring societies; and now, in not much more than half a century, has come to be universally established, and to be regarded, next to the church, a mighty lever with which to move the world. We, who are or have been inhabitants of this town, have been accustomed, not without some show of reason, to pride ourselves on several first things that are interwoven with its history. The first vessel, which, at the commencement of the Revolution, unfurled the Continental flag, and went forth, in defiance of British domination, to brave the mistress of the seas, sailed hence. Here the infant American navy was born and cradled; William Bartlett, after whom one of your pleasantest streets is named, having been the first commissioned navy agent. Here the first cotton-factory in America was established. Here, too, was organized the first lyceum for debate and lectures, which, in some form or another, has spread through the length and breadth of the land. But who of us — certainly not I — will question, that the best first, or first best, whichever way you may please to put it, on which we congratulate ourselves and each other, is — when viewed in all its aspects and bearings on society and the human soul — the parish Sunday school? Of this parent school, Robert Rantoul, so well known and highly esteemed in church and State, — who long, from experience and acknowledged ability, wielded an influence second to that of few, if any, in our State; and whose name, by the offices he filled and the services he rendered in this church and parish, must ever be identified with them, — was the first superintendent, and always the ardent and consistent supporter. Nothing could be more characteristic of the unflagging interest he felt in its objects, and of the spirit of the man, than the following entry in his diary, occasioned by a recent attendance at a sabbath-school convention : —

" The occasion has been one of healthful excitement and enjoyment to me. The more than thirty years that I was connected with the Sunday school in this parish, give an example of perseverance in an attempt to do good, however numerous were my shortcomings, that may have its just influence with some others to induce them to hold out and hold on, although the good result of their labors may not be very apparent. Progress, if slow but certain, will ultimately confer its own best reward, in the reflection that we have tried to do good, and that we have persevered in our best endeavors as long as circumstances would justify it. My resolutions are strengthened by this occasion."

And this was written at or near the close of his seventy-eighth year.

Here I must pause. It would ill become me to speak of the ministry which succeeded that of the revered Abbot. For you, and not for me, is it to say how far you were harmonized in doctrine, established in sacred and everlasting truth, led to the observance of the commandments and ordinances; how far, in

short, under it and by it the great ends of religion have been
answered; namely, the upholding and extending of good institutions, the promotion of piety and pure morals, of universal
reform and progress. It will always be to me a pleasant and
precious memory, that the sacred trust, which for more than a
quarter of a century you reposed in me, was given back with —
so far as I know or have heard — no mutual censures or reproach, but in entire reciprocal concord. Whatever may have
been my deficiencies or failures in duty and usefulness, I acknowledge with unfeigned sensibility the candid construction
and kind judgment you have uniformly hitherto extended to
them in my lifetime; not doubting, moreover, that, when I
am gone, those of you who shall survive me will tread lightly
on my ashes, and tenderly guard — it may be, cherish — my
memory.

What my successor has accomplished and may expect to
accomplish, what may be hoped by, for, and of him, in the consecrated relation you and he sustain, it might be unseemly in
me, before his and your presence, to declare or predict. Still,
I will not forbear congratulating him and yourselves on this
society's present condition and prospects; on its union, firmness,
and zeal in maintaining what I regard, and from the first advo-
cated among you, as the most pure and the best form and doctrine of Christianity yet attained, — those of Unitarianism; and
now, especially, on the spirit exhibited in the renovated and
beautified aspect of this temple; trusting, at the same time, that
you and he will be ever mindful, that the most beauteous and
holy of temples on earth is the purified and sanctified soul of
man, infinitely exceeding in grandeur and beauty all gracefully
turned and lofty arches, all frescoed walls, or material splendor.

We have dwelt much and long, and with, I hope, a pardon-
able exultation, on the labors and worth of them who have preceded us. Of our worthy predecessors we may well exclaim,
keeping in view also the uncertainties that cast their shadow on
all human life and experience, —

> " 'Tis well with them.
> But who knows what the coming hour,
> Veiled in thick darkness, brings for us ? "

Amid all shades, however, of uncertainty and vicissitude that may surround the path before us, we should rejoice that duty only is ours, and that events are with God alone. Let us work while the day of life lasts, be it longer or shorter, in well-doing as universal and thorough as may be in our power. Never before, in all the series of ages past, was such a plane afforded for human exertion. Earth and the heavens are all aglow with the light of new discoveries, new means of physical, intellectual, moral, and religious improvement, — with ideas, old and new, of truth, liberty, justice, love, holiness, and heaven. What better counsel could I, in addressing you of this society collectively, for possibly — I had almost said probably — the last time, leave with you or take to myself, than that we should be faithful to our great trusts, seize the moments of precious privilege as they fly, and improve to the utmost our golden opportunity for the soul's enlargement and elevation, for being and doing good, and so securing for ourselves and many others — how many eternity only can reveal — real and highest felicity ? If only we are true to our high vocation, our sacred obligations, and vast opportunities, act well the sublime part Providence has assigned to us of this generation, we shall live honored and die lamented ; we shall constitute a not inglorious link between the past and coming centuries ; our spirit shall be diffused in good influences through the ages that are to come ; and future generations will rise up and call us blessed.

ORDER OF EXERCISES

ON THE

TWO-HUNDREDTH ANNIVERSARY

OF THE

First Parish, Beverly.

VOLUNTARY AND CHORAL.

INTRODUCTORY PRAYER.

ANTHEM.

SELECTIONS FROM THE BIBLE.

ORIGINAL HYMN.

Give glory to the Holy One,
Who dwelleth not in heaven alone,
Nor scorneth humble work well done,
Though high exalted is His throne ;
To Him our hearts would still upraise
A church, a monument of praise.

Defying time, despite all change,
And grateful as the dew to flowers,
The records of His mercy range
O'er all the varied, fleeting hours.
While felt His might and owned His sway,
Two hundred years have passed away.

What are we, who so long have known
A habitation and a name !
One meek and lowly guide we own,
" One God, one faith, one baptism " claim.
We gratefully the past review ;
Our God is love, and ever true.

MARY E. WORSLEY.

————

PRAYER.

————

ORIGINAL HYMN.

" Lo, I am with you alway even to the end." — MATT. xxviii. 20.

E'EN to the end, the Master said,
　I will be with you ; and to-day
The Church responds to her great Head,
　Thou hast been with us, Lord, — alway.

Alway — through these two hundred years,
　Alway — upon this holy ground
Made sacred by the feet of saints,
　Who their eternal rest have found.

Alway — to keep undimmed the faith,
　The blessed faith we have in thee,
Alway — to make its heaven-born truth
　More broad, more beautiful, and free.

Through time and change, through life and death,
　We still upon thy promise stand,
Strong in Thy strength, as stood of yore
　The fathers of our sainted band.

Like them, we seek to wash our robes ;
　Like them, to do our Master's will.
God grant us faith and hope and love,
　And Thy abiding presence still.

EMILY O. KIMBALL.

————

HISTORICAL ADDRESS,
BY REV. C. T. THAYER, OF BOSTON.

————

DOXOLOGY.
" FROM ALL THAT DWELL BELOW THE SKIES."

————

BENEDICTION.

After the services at the Church, an elegant and sumptuous dinner, at which Dr. W. C. BOYDEN presided, was served at the Town Hall; and the festivities of the occasion were continued with animated and interesting remarks by various gentlemen of the Parish and from abroad, singing by the choir, and the reading of a poem.

The following original Hymn was sung in the course of the afternoon : —

THE sea made music to the shore
   Two hundred years ago ;
To weary pilgrim ears it bore
   A prelude deep and low.

They gathered, in the Autumn calm,
   To their new house of prayer,
And softly rose their Sabbath psalm,
   A blessing on the air.

The ocean took the echo up ;
   It rang through every tree ;
And praise, as from an incense cup,
   Filled earth and sky and sea.

They linger yet upon the breeze,
   The hymns our fathers sung ;
They rustle in the wayside trees,
   And give each leaf a tongue.

The murmuring sea is burdened yet
   With music's mighty pain ;
No fitting chorus men have set
   To that great organ-strain.

When human hearts are tuned to Thine,
   Whose voice is in the sea,
Life's moaning waves a song divine
   Shall swell, O God, to Thee !

LUCY LARCOM.

11